D1758125

CRIME SCENE ASIA

CRIME SCENE ASIA

VOL.1

RICHARD LORD
(Editor)

monsoon

monsoonbooks

Published in 2013
by Monsoon Books Pte Ltd
71 Ayer Rajah Crescent #01-01, Singapore 139951
www.monsoonbooks.com.sg

ISBN (print): 978-981-4423-33-5
ISBN (ebook): 978-981-4423-34-2

Cover design by Cover Kitchen.

National Library Board, Singapore Cataloguing-in-Publication Data
Crime scene Asia. Vol. 1 / Richard Lord, editor. – Singapore : Monsoon Books
Pte Ltd, 2013.
pages cm
ISBN : 978-981-4423-33-5 (paperback)

1. Detective and mystery stories, English – Asia. 2. Short stories, Oriental (English) I. Lord, Richard A. (Richard Alan)

PR9418
828.9950301 -- dc23   OCN852767335

Printed in Singapore
15 14 13   1 2 3 4 5

Contents

INTRODUCTION   9

Thailand
You Get What You Pay For by Elka Ray   15
Lord Tony's Deal by Roger Vickery   33
Wet Nightmares by Jim Algie   57

Singapore
November Rain by D. Biswas   83
Road Kill by Richard Lord   99

Malaysia
The Cat City Caper by Dawn Farnham   143

Philippines
On A Wet Day You Can Live Forever by Charlson Ong   157

India
The Case of The Too Many Fingerprints by Abha Iyengar   175

Vietnam
The Hanoi Sword Swindle by William L. Gibson   191

AUTHOR COPYRIGHTS   228
CONTRIBUTE TO CRIME SCENE ASIA   228

Introduction

Like most struggling authors, I am addicted to the Amazon.com Book Bestsellers List. After a painful regime of withdrawal, I've stopped consulting the lists every waking hour, and I can now sometimes go a few days without surveying the Top 100, trying to see what's really selling, what the latest reading trends are, trying to predict the next trends, all in the hopes of rising out of that 'struggling author' status.

For the last two years, there have been two major trends in these bestseller rosters, especially in the fiction field. One is the bondage-as-the-path-to-freedom novel epitomised by the *Fifty Shades* and *Entwined* series and their heavily panting imitators. The other is the continuing popularity, if not dominance, of crime fiction titles.

The vast popularity of these two forms should not be too surprising. Crime is as inevitable and as deeply rooted in the human experience as sex itself. Like sex, it's a subject that touches a deep part of us, that fascinates us, that clicks buttons inside us and makes us want more. And even more than sex, the subject of crime gets us asking questions and seeking answers. Clearly, some of the most interesting (often troubling) questions and more compelling answers are found in the realm of crime fiction.

While some uninformed types may see crime fiction as an

inferior literary genre, I would argue that it is, in fact, a serious and important genre because it often engages with what are literally life-and-death issues. In a world where the lines between the legal and illegal have grown distressingly thin, where more and more, we find ourselves stumbling about in moral grey zones, no serious reader can ignore the importance of crime fiction.

As crime remains an enduring presence in our world, crime fiction's popularity seems assured for the near and medium future. As Asia is also a central focus of many all around the world these days, the conjunction of Asia and crime fiction seemed a very natural development. And thus this book.

For this first volume of Crime Scene Asia, I have selected nine stories by nine different authors that cover a wide multitude of crimes, as well as a broad range of literary styles, characters and milieus. Murder mystery fans will certainly get their fix here, as will as those who appreciate the why-dunit as much as the standard whodunit.

In these pages, we witness robberies of precious objects, smuggling of various commodities legal and not so legal. There are also stories about robbery for revenge, revenge killings, and extreme cruelty just for the fun of it – or to escape deep existential boredom.

A major reason behind my selection of the stories in this volume was to gather a diversity of styles and visions for this initial volume. For instance, I was immediately taken by the wry, dark humour infusing two of the pieces (Cat City Caper and You Get What You Pay For). But I was also seduced by the bitter innocence of the narrator and central protagonist in Jim Algie's Wet Nightmares. And I will admit that I'm a sucker for crime stories where you not really sure who is the main criminal, who is the accomplice and who is the victim. (Sometimes you're still not sure at the end of the story.) Which is why I was enthusiastic about fine pieces such as Hanoi Sword Swindle, Lord Tony's Deal and On A Wet Day You Can Live Forever.

I think that most lovers of crime fiction will find much to please them in this collection. For those who are enamoured of the time-honoured detective stories, there are three solid pieces here, though Charlson's Ong's On A Wet Day is anything but the traditional detective story that we see in The Case of the Too Many Fingerprints or Road Kill. As editor, I was happy to include the conventional, well-constructed detective story as well as Ong's creative deconstruction of that genre.

As a reader – and an editor – what particularly draws me to stories is not just good stories but compelling characters. In fact, my final selection of the nine stories in this volume was made because of the characters that enliven the plots and the settings. Whether criminal, victim, detective, or accomplice, the people we meet in these pages engage us right from the start and keep us interested in them and their predicaments, their fates until the last sentence of each story. Many of the leading characters presented here – especially those on the wrong side of the law – are probably not folks you would want to spend a lot of time with, but you don't want to leave them until their tales have fully played out.

Of course, Aristotle told us over two millennia ago that a character is defined by the action he or she is either thrown into or pursues. And that's why the characters in these stories are so compelling: they pursue criminal activities or they pursue those who commit crimes. And not a few of these characters are thrown into situations they would not have chosen themselves and try to work their way out the best they can.

As the plots are spun out, the characters are tested and so more sharply defined. We know them, or we realise they are mysteries no one can ever really know. By the end of each story, there is something like just desserts, even when the desserts are rather bitter.

Finally, I believe that this volume is a fine introduction to the state of crime, and pursuit of criminals, in six leading Asian countries. It is a good beginning to what promises to be an excellent series.

Richard Lord

Thailand

YOU GET WHAT YOU PAY FOR

ELKA RAY

Nobody in their right mind would fly all the way to Thailand only to shop in Prada, but that's exactly what Candice is doing. She could buy the same stuff back home for less money, since imported luxury goods are heavily taxed here. But, of course, she's not looking at the price tags. I'm sitting in Starbucks waiting for her, and we've been in this mall for more than three hours already.

It's a high-end place, the customers falling into two categories: bewildered-looking tourists in cheap, un-ironed clothes and immaculately turned-out Thai ladies who lunch, all of whom seem to be toting small dogs and five-thousand-dollar handbags.

A few of these ladies' husbands are sitting near me in Starbucks, killing time on their mobiles and iPads. I see the guy at the next table check his Rolex and frown. Moments later, his perfectly-coiffed wife appears, trailing two giant Hermes bags.

I check my own watch. Where the hell is Candice?

When I spot her, I'm torn between dismay and relief. On the one hand, we can finally get out of this mall. On the other, she is carrying two large LV bags. Spending money – my money – does something to Candice's brain, releases serotonin or something. She pecks me on the cheek and takes a seat, her face frozen into the glazed, giddy look that toddlers get when they've had too much sugar.

'I found the cutest shoes ever,' she says. 'Do you want to see them?'

I've lived with Candice long enough to know that saying 'no' is not an option. Sure enough, she's already pried open the box and extracted some layers of tissue paper. I drain the last of my double-espresso.

'What do you think?' says Candice.

My wife is a beautiful woman, a former Miss Teen Texas. When I met her, she was stunning. In photos, she looks almost as good as she used to, but in real life, up close, the effort that's gone into maintaining her looks is unmistakable. I'm not sure what it is, because she's never overdone the plastic surgery, but it's like the difference between a real flower and a fake one.

'Martin?' says Candice.

I realize that I'd failed to respond to her question. 'Nice,' I say. 'Yeah, those are quite something.'

They are something, just not something I'd want my wife to be spending my money on – a pair of red, strappy sandals that are ludicrously high. There's no way that Candice can walk in those things.

Candice pouts, her already plumped lips jutting out by a few more millimetres. 'You don't like them,' she says.

I fight down a sigh. 'I do like them,' I say. 'You're going to look hot in those.'

I refrain from asking how much they cost. Candice and I are going to be in Thailand for another week. While I don't expect to enjoy myself, I may as well make the best of things. If I see the price tags on those shoes, I'm likely to say something that'll lead to an argument.

After I've admired her other shoes too – flashy silver sandals that are equally high – Candice goes off to order a skim-milk cappuccino. I try not to look, but a corner of the receipt is sticking out from a shoe bag. While I don't allow myself to do the currency conversion, one glance at all of those zeros gives me instant heartburn.

It's not that I'm poor. It's the principle. I'm a corporate lawyer and a partner in a big Houston firm: Burton, Gottgart, Gillard & Associates. But in the words of Dolly Parton, I work hard for my money.

'I got you this,' says Candice. She sets a square of industrial-looking carrot cake in front of me. I know that she'll allow herself a couple of bites but no more. I'm not hungry, but pick up the fork anyway.

The cream-cheese icing isn't bad. Candice is describing all of the other items that she'd considered buying. I listen just enough to be able to nod at the right places, a skill that I mastered at work, decades ago. As Candice talks about this season's must-have colors and skirt lengths, I fantasize about Brittany, the new receptionist at Burton, Gottgart, Gillard &

Associates. I started sleeping with her two months ago, and it's still in the fresh and exciting phase. While I don't actually miss Brittany, I do miss having sex with her. She's a nice enough girl, just fairly dull … outside of the bedroom.

This is a pattern with me.

Back before I made partner, Candice was the receptionist at Burton & Gottgart. I was still married to my fist wife, Patty, with whom I have two sons, Karl and Martin Junior. They're both in boarding school in New England. It's costing me a fortune.

'They had some cute swimsuits in Prada,' says Candice. 'There were these white bikinis with little gold chains holding everything together.'

'Oh yeah?' I say. Candice needs more swimsuits like she needs more Botox. Or like she needs more thousand-dollar shoes, for that matter.

'Uh huh, but they didn't have my size.'

Well thank God for that, I think. Then I imagine Brittany in a tiny white bikini. I picture her wriggling out of it. She's nowhere near as pretty as either of my wives, but her tits are a whole lot bigger. They're real too. I guess that's what I miss about her.

'Martin?' Candice has the pinched look that she gets when she's pissed at me. 'You weren't listening,' she says. 'We finally get to spend some time together, and you aren't even paying attention to me.'

Contrition seems easier than denial. 'Sorry,' I say. I set down my fork and stage a yawn. 'I think it's jetlag. How about we go back to the hotel?' Sex with Candice would be better than nothing.

'Just come with me and look in Armani,' says Candice brightly. 'They're having a sale. It'll only take a minute.'

I tell her that I'll wait here. Candice promises to be quick. I retrieve the newspaper left by the guy with the Rolex.

I've made it to page five, and there's still no sign of Candice. At the bottom of the page, there's a short item about an Australian tourist who'd been found dead the previous week on Koh Phangan. Apparently, a young guy by the name of Jason Duncan Peal had gotten drunk and waded, fully-clothed, into the sea and drowned. It's been ruled an accident.

What catches my attention is how the story ends:

Mr Peal is the fourth foreign national to have died on the island this month, with two of the other fatalities having been attributed to drug overdoses and the third to unknown causes. Meanwhile, it is thought that a Belgian woman found dead in a Koh Samui hotel two days ago committed suicide.

That's five dead tourists in three weeks, in beach destinations that are marketed as tropical paradise. Candice and I are headed to the beach in two days' time. Maybe Thailand's not as safe as I thought it was.

The next morning, at breakfast, I read *The Bangkok Post*. On page four, I find yet another short story about the suspicious death of a foreign tourist.

Police in Chiang Mai have confirmed that a 27-year-old Dutch woman was found dead in her room at the Golden Dragon Hotel on Monday morning. While autopsy results are still pending, severe food poisoning is suspected.

This woman, whose name has yet to be released, is the third guest at the Golden Dragon Hotel to have died under mysterious circumstances in the past year. Last March, a

65-year-old Danish man died in his room of apparent food poisoning following a buffet breakfast. In July, a 43-year-old female Thai tour guide was found dead in a hotel bathroom after complaining of stomach cramps.

In a statement issued to the press yesterday, a Chiang Mai police spokesman said: 'There is absolutely no evidence to suggest that these cases are related.'

I set down the piece of pineapple that I'd been eating. Pre-cut fruit could be deadly. I shake my head. Three dead tourists in one hotel and the cops think it's a coincidence! What kind of investigations are these bozos running? True, we're in a five-star hotel and the Golden Dragon is probably a shit-hole, but it still makes me scared to eat anything.

'What's the matter?' says Candice. She is holding a large plate bearing a single croissant. Surrounded by gleaming whiteness, the pastry looks small and sad, like a child's drawing of a frown.

I realize that I'm frowning too. 'Agh, just the news,' I say. I fold up the paper. 'It's the same shit everywhere.'

Candice puts down her plate and takes a seat. 'Are you going to eat that pineapple?' she says. I tell her to go ahead. I'm going to stick to bananas.

The next day's *Bangkok Post* is even worse. I read it on the plane to Krabi. There are three separate stories, all of them short, but what it boils down to is four dead tourists in less than twenty-four hours: a 64 year-old Australian man found dead in an alley in Bangkok (drugs suspected, possibly not self-administered); a 31-year-old Nigerian man stabbed, also in Bangkok; and two Japanese drowning victims near Phuket, one a 21-year-old woman and the other her 23-year-old male companion.

Am I here at an unusually unlucky time? Or is this normal?

It's not until my untouched in-flight meal has been cleared away that the idea comes to me. At first, it's just a crazy idea. But the more that I think about it, the more sense it makes.

I am 49 years old. Candice is 38. We both have a lot of years ahead of us.

I research the drugs on the Internet. There's a pharmacy about a block from our resort. In Thailand, no prescriptions are necessary. Of course, it's a risk to buy the stuff so close to where we're staying, but I haven't gotten to where I am in my life without taking chances. As it turns out, the teenage girl behind the counter is too busy watching a Chinese soap to even look at me. She grabs the stuff that I've listed without removing her eyes from the screen, like she's a blind person moving by instinct and touch. Even still, I am shaking when I hand over the money.

After that, I wait. I'm still not sure that I'll do it. It's one thing to think about something like that, and another to act on it. But Candice is driving me crazy.

Thailand is too hot for my liking, but I have to admit that the scenery around here is fantastic, with steep limestone islands as jagged as sharks' teeth. Me and Candice are set to explore them in rented kayaks. We'd planned to leave around 3 pm, but then Candice had insisted on getting a pedicure. By the time that we get into our kayaks, it's well past four. Luckily, the sun's not as intense as it was.

'Are you sure we don't need a guide?' says Candice. She is wearing a tiny bikini and a massive sunhat.

'What for?' I say. 'We'll just paddle around and stop on an empty beach somewhere.' Stowed in my kayak is a picnic hamper. I've even brought a flask of Candice's favorite cocktail, a vicious mix of apricot brandy, gin, dry vermouth and lime juice.

Because all of the resorts around here are high-end, the beach is relatively empty. The bay is empty too, with just a few windsurfers visible down at the far end. The water is the same color as my swimming pool.

It is late afternoon and the light has an incredible golden quality to it. We paddle towards the limestone islands. Everything – including Candice – looks more beautiful than it is. Looking at her tanned skin and expertly streaked hair, I almost love her again. Then she opens her mouth and ruins everything.

'This is hard,' she says. 'I think we should go back. We're not getting anywhere.'

I have to admit that paddling is tougher than it looks. We must be battling a current. 'Not far now,' I say. 'Just think of how many calories you're burning.'

About twenty minutes – and as many complaints – later, we reach the first of the limestone islands. Up close, they look fairly creepy, with sheer, dark grey walls that tower over us like ruined castles. Paddling between them, we are in deep shade. It's like entering a cave, the temperature noticeably cooler.

In the narrow channels between the islands, paddling is harder still. We're getting tossed around. It's a relief to round an island and see a stretch of open sea, and a deserted, sunny beach facing towards it. 'Let's stop,' says Candice. 'My arms are going to be so sore tomorrow.'

When the water is waist-deep, we both dive in. It feels good to rinse the sweat off. After pulling the kayaks up onto the sand, I retrieve the picnic basket.

'I'm so thirsty,' says Candice.

Of course, I have a choice. And of course, I know that what I'm about to do is wrong. Candice may be shallow, materialistic, petty and mind-bogglingly boring, but she's not a terrible person. She doesn't deserve to die. But since when was life fair? And I have to think of myself here.

I'm 49. I plan to be around for another three decades. And I really don't want to spend them with Candice. But if I divorce her, she gets a huge settlement. It was bad enough with Patty, and I was worth a whole lot less back then. Just the thought of Candy walking off with half of my assets makes my blood pressure jump.

I grab the glasses and fill them. And then, when Candice is looking at the view, I sprinkle the powder in hers.

'To freedom,' I say. We clink glasses. I try not to watch as she takes a sip, but can't help myself.

She makes a face. 'This tastes different.'

'It's the limes,' I say. 'Back home, we use lemons.'

'Mmm. It's not as good.'

I nod. 'Try drinking it quickly.'

It takes about twenty minutes to see an effect. We are both lying on the sand watching the sunset. 'Candice?' I say, but there is no response. My wife is sleeping.

She might, of course, just be taking a nap. I shake her gently, then do it harder. Ten minutes later, when I'm sure that she's really out, I push her kayak into the water. I rinse out our glasses and the flask, then set them by the water's edge. The tide is coming in.

Before going to pick up Candice, I go over my story one last time. Candice went out for a paddle while I took a nap. I woke to find her empty kayak floating offshore. Candice can swim, but she's not a strong swimmer. I didn't hear a thing. Yes, she'd been drinking.

After that, I go to pick up Candice, along with her massive hat and her Chanel glasses. She seems heavier than usual, but she's still pretty light. Which isn't surprising, considering how little she eats.

I am at the water's edge when I hear something. Rounding the corner of the island is an open-decked, long-tailed boat. They must have just turned their engine on.

I freeze. The boat comes closer. On board are an old Thai driver and four Western kids. I can make out three guys and one girl. They look around my sons' age.

'Hey mister! Is everything okay?' yells one of the guys. Dressed in nothing but a pair of ragged pink cotton pants, he has a head-full of filthy-looking blond dreadlocks. The girl, meanwhile, has a crew cut. I was tipped off to her gender by small tits in a crochet bikini.

The boat slows. My heart is pounding so fast that I'm scared that something will rattle loose in there. Candice is still lying limp in my arms. For once, I am speechless. I drop the sunhat.

I take a deep breath. 'I ... I ... Help!' I yell. 'Something has happened to my wife!'

The kid with the dreadlocks hops overboard and splashes towards us. 'It's okay!' he yells. 'I'm a doctor!'

I can't fucking believe it. Is this kid really old enough to be a doctor?

I set Candice down, and he leans over her, then applies a finger to her neck. I catch a whiff of pot mixed with coconut-scented sunscreen. But despite his youth, and all of the weed that he's obviously inhaled, the kid seems to know what he's doing. I watch glumly as he checks her pulse.

'Let's lift her,' he says. I want to punch the guy.

Aided by the rest of the gang, we lift Candice onto the boat. I climb in after her. The deck is littered with snorkels, diving equipment and bags of junk food. Sure enough, a bong lies near the prow. I could use a good hit. My heart is still racing.

The driver starts the engine. 'Hold on,' he yells. This is not a figure of speech. We are moving so fast that I'm scared for my life. With each wave that we hit, I imagine the boat flying apart. Candice is lucky to be out of it.

She's lucky to miss the taxi ride too, and the sight of the crowds milling out front of the local hospital. Luckily for her, there's a special, overpriced ward where they treat foreigners. She ends up having her stomach pumped.

Not surprisingly, when she's released from the hospital, Candice wants to go home. I try to convince her that it was food poisoning, but some Thai doctor suggested that she might have been drugged. Naturally, she freaked out.

So now, we're back in the same hotel in Bangkok. Our return flight to Houston is tomorrow morning.

'How did I get drugged?' says Candice, for about the hundredth time. She is lying on a white sofa with her slutty red sandals on. Even though it's not my sofa, this drives me crazy.

Why can't she take her filthy shoes off?

'It must have happened at the resort,' I say. 'Maybe someone tried to drug both of us. At the buffet, maybe. It could have been a failed robbery or something.'

Candice shudders. 'We should have gone to the police. I almost died,' she says. She downs the last of her gin and tonic.

I shudder too. If that boatload of stoners had rounded the corner just a few seconds later, they'd have seen me trying to drown my wife. On the other hand, if Candice hadn't insisted on getting that stupid pedicure, everything would have worked out perfectly. I was so close.

Fighting down a sigh, I stand up to fix us fresh drinks. When will I get another good opportunity to get rid of Candice?

'We should have gone to Hawaii,' says Candice. She sticks out her lip. 'I hate this place.'

Since it was her idea to come here, she can't blame me, but I know that she wants to. When Candice drinks, she gets argumentative. And tonight, she's drunk a fair bit. We both have, but I'm a lot bigger than Candice.

'We can go for Christmas,' I say soothingly. Maybe Candice can fall from some steep mountain trail, or get pulled out to sea by a rip tide. But even as I think it, I know that it's a bad idea. Hawaii has a modern police force. I wouldn't dare try anything suspicious in a place that produced something like *Hawaii Five-O*. 'Life in jail' has a nasty ring to it. And back in Texas, I could even be looking at the death penalty.

'Or how about Mexico?' I say. Mexico would be okay. Everyone knows that the cops there are corrupt and useless.

'Hawaii,' says Candice firmly. 'Or Florida.'

I ask if she wants another drink, then extract two tiny

bottles of gin and a can of tonic from the mini-bar. It'll be at least another year before Candice agrees to go any place more exotic than Honolulu. Having had freedom so close, I can't help but feel bitter. I grab another bottle of gin and top up both of our glasses.

When I carry the drinks back to the couch, I see that Candice has gone out onto the balcony. She's leaned up against the railing admiring the view. I walk out to join her.

We're on the sixteenth floor, dotted lines of traffic snaking far below. In the distance, I can see the bell roof of a *wat*, shining gold in its floodlights.

Candice takes the drink without saying 'thank you'. She takes a sip, then informs me that I've put too much tonic in it.

'You're drunk,' I say. 'That's why you can't taste the alcohol.'

She tosses her hair. 'I am not drunk,' she says. 'Taste this! There's practically no gin in there.' She thrusts the glass towards me.

I know that Candice is drunk and that I should let this go. But I'm angry. 'I poured it myself,' I say. 'So what, you're calling me a liar?'

Candice narrows her eyes. 'Don't get me started,' she says.

Candice is tall and, in her new sandals, she's even taller. The balcony railing is low. It'd never meet building codes back home. But I guess that most Asians are short. It must have been built to meet local standards.

'What's that supposed to mean?' I say.

Candice sways on her feet. 'You're so cheap, you probably poured half a shot to keep the mini-bar tab down.'

'Cheap?' I say. 'Who's paying for this hotel, Candice? Who

paid for our flights, and all of that designer shit that you're wearing, and your new tits and lips and everything else for that matter?'

Candice opens her mouth, then shuts it. I'm not usually that crude, or that blunt, but I'm too angry to sugarcoat things. I finish the last of my gin and tonic. Candice is still glaring at me. Any second now, I bet she'll start crying.

Instead, she tells me to fuck off. 'You think I don't know about you and that little slag Brittany?' She laughs, or rather a strange gurgle comes out of her throat, half laugh and half cry. Her fat mouth looks twisted and ugly.

I am shocked. I didn't think that she knew. Why hasn't she said anything?

Candice's strangled laugh comes again. She has twisted around so that her back is to the view. She's got one elbow on the rail and her glass in the other hand. It occurs to me that she might toss her drink at me.

'I knew,' she says. 'And you know what? That bitch can have you. I want a divorce.' She bares her capped teeth at me. 'On the grounds of adultery.'

I set down my empty glass. Has Candice been collecting proof of my affair to increase her settlement? All of a sudden, I feel totally sober.

I swallow hard. It's time for damage control. 'Aw, come on baby. Don't be like that.' I lean forward to touch her arm. Candice has many faults, but holding grudges has never been one of them. She's caught me cheating before.

'I'll make it up to you,' I say, blinking real tears into my eyes. 'I'll ... I'll go to couples counselling, or do whatever you want. Anything!' I take a step closer and reach for her chin.

'You know I can't live without you.'

She smiles, and for a moment, I think she's come round, but then there's a sharp pain in my shin. I stumble back. 'Ow!' I yell. The little bitch just kicked me!

I look down in time to see her shiny red foot lash out again, but can't move fast enough to avoid it. This kick hits me in the left knee, causing me to gasp in pain. Candy throws back her head and laughs, her long blonde hair swaying over the rail.

'You bastard!' she says, and I see her foot recoil for another blow. This time, I manage to jump out of the way and grab hold of her sandal, Candy balanced like a teeter-totter until one upward tug sends those red shoes skyward.

While our fight had happened very fast, she seems to fall in slow motion.

I threaten to sue the hotel, on account of their railing being so low, but don't plan to go through with it. It's an international hotel chain, but the case would be tried in Thailand. I figure that it's not worth the effort. Naturally, they raise all of the balcony railings and fix the banisters too. They also put up signs warning guests not to sit on the edges of their balconies, to cover their asses against possible litigation in case of future accidents.

The autopsy results show that Candy had a blood alcohol level of 0.24. Her death is deemed an accident. It warrants a brief story in the *Bangkok Post*, but is overshadowed by the auto-asphyxiation of a minor, has-been British pop singer in a hotel room in Pattaya.

Rather than pay to have Candice's body shipped back to Texas, I opt to have her cremated in Bangkok, then repatriate her ashes. This saves me a ton of money.

* * *

Back in Houston, I take Candice's ashes to her favourite mall, The Galleria. Like usual at this time of year, it's hotter than hell, but there's a decent breeze. I sprinkle her ashes outside of Saks, just a little at a time, since I don't want to attract attention.

Standing out there in the parking lot with my empty urn, I can't help but feel a little nostalgic. After all, Candice did have her good points. We'd had some fun times together. Since I don't know what else to do with it, I hide the urn in a planter.

I'm getting back into my Porsche when I feel something tap me on the shoulder. I spin around, but there's no one there. Must be my guilty conscience, because I also catch a whiff of Candy's favorite Chanel perfume. I have to admit that I'm rattled.

But then I tell myself to get a grip. Candice is dead, and that's all there is to it. I start the engine and crank the air con. Ghosts, God, karma – they're all a bunch of horseshit. I believe in the here-and-now, and right now, I'm a free man. I crank the stereo.

Maybe I'm driving a little faster than usual, but I see the light change with plenty of time to stop, except that when I tap the brake, the car accelerates. There's a loud screech and the blast of a truck horn, panic causing me to stamp on the brake. Still, the Porsche lurches onwards. I don't understand. Am I pressing the wrong pedal?

I look down, struggling to make sense of it, the smell of

Candy's perfume so strong that it's hard to breathe. I see a flash of red down near my feet, the same shiny red as Candice's sandals, the same red that shatters inside my head and runs into my eyes until everything fades to blackness.

Elka Ray (*www.elkaray.com*) is the author of one novel, *Hanoi Jane*, and two kids' books about Vietnam, which she also illustrated. Born in England and raised in Canada, Elka has spent the past 17 years in Vietnam. She adores mysteries, tropical oceans and dark humour.

Thailand

LORD TONY'S DEAL

ROGER VICKERY

Every long-term *farang* called him Lord Tony, even the ones who thought he was a compete fraud. All I knew for certain about his past was that his family lived at Batworthy-on-the-Moor, Kestor Rock, Batworthy, South Devon. That was the return address on the letters I collected for him from the Bangkok post office. Tony refused to appear in the city in daylight, and he was very keen that his residence was not listed on any official data base.

Playing delivery boy for Lord Tony was a pleasure. He had charm, a compound overflowing with jade and orchids, and this new housemaid called Thuy. She was sitting below Tony, her feet pointing away from him as Thai custom demands, translating for a jade dealer in soft GI English.

'He say, "Don't screw this, Joe. This best gear. Border fuzz give him too many hassle. So if you do same, it's *so long baby*." '

Tony was giving his impression of Rodin's *Thinker*, nodding and then drawling appropriate replies.

'I see. Thank you, darling. Would you tell my good buddy Mister Cheong that I appreciate his difficulties. Or rather, I get his hassles, but it's tough titty. I like him as a guy, but I can only offer – I mean hit him with – 20,000 baht.'

A tank of pinkish, scarlet-speckled orchids framed Thuy's profile as she kept her eyes respectfully low, only raising them when it was her turn to talk. Her nose, which was flatter and wider than the southern Thais appreciate, gave her face a strength I wasn't used to seeing in local girls. The wider brow and the dark brown skin confirmed her Burmese blood.

Tony had moaned to me about this maid, 'She speaks six dialects; she's intelligent, industrious, very pretty and unwilling to go to bed for less than two buffaloes.'

Some poor farmers from the north will trade their daughters to Bangkok merchants for a good water buffalo. The girls are supposed to return home in a few years, but once they climb into the Mercedes, they rarely see the paddy fields again.

Thuy had absconded from the Chinese businessman who had paid his buffalo to her father, so she could never go home. She lived with a Yank pilot for a while. After he was posted to Manila, she had worked in bars and then somehow ended up at Tony's compound.

During a pause in the negotiations, I saw Thuy aim an icy stare at Tony. My hunch was that her price for him was always going to be one buffalo too high.

'Like a glass of Mekong?' I asked her. Most Thai girls would giggle at such an embarrassing question. Women do the serving, and they aren't supposed to drink working man's liquor. Thuy simply smiled a refusal.

As soon as the dealer had been *wai'd* out of the room, Tony had made a beeline for the letters I'd brought. Winning the body-language duel with the dealer had put him in a good mood. By keeping his head and clasped hands a millimetre higher than Cheong's *wai,* Tony had won the all-important body language duel. Humming, he picked up the letter bearing the Batworthy crest and held it to the light as if was a piece of dubious jade.

'I'll read this with the help of my opium pipe. It's the only company possible when dealing with father – it's migraine country otherwise. Thuy will look after you. I'm sure she'll enjoy your etchings. *Arrivederci.*'

Tony knew I kept a journal – a sketchpad with jottings, quotes and colourful mementos. It's cheaper than opium, and it helps me to kid myself that there's more to me than forging passports and visas.

'Ettings. What they?' asked Thuy.

I reached into my daypack and produced the calf-bound accounts ledger that served as my current journal. Thuy spent a long time over each page, praising every sketch, sounding out strange words and running her fingers over the unusual visuals, like the feathers and matchbox covers stuck onto some pages.

'You *adjan.* Got egghead ...' She tapped her brow and then laid her hand on a firm left breast. 'Got big heart.'

An *adjan* is a teacher, a wise man. The Thais revere education. Whenever I've been scribbling away, most Thais, the poorer ones anyway, have treated me with genuine respect, which is more than they give to most *farangs*.

I showed Thuy a crayon sketch of a dancer I had copied from an ancient mural on the wall of a *wat* in the northeast corner near Burma.

'Must be your great, great, great grandmother,' I teased. 'See: same face, hands.' *And breasts*, I thought. Thuy arched her fingers and bent her long v-shaped nails back almost far enough to brush the back of her hands. She slid her face behind them, veiling her eyes, copying the expectant pose of the temple dancer. After we had locked eyes for long enough, I made the next move. 'How do you reckon your granny would feel about a smoke?'

* * *

A pack of Norfolk hounds snapping at a fox flew past my nose and shattered against the wall. I looked up and saw that it was Tony who had thrown the hunting print, and it was Tony who was standing over me.

'Are you ... uh ... a bit pissed off, mate, about Thuy and me breaking out your best Buddha?' I ventured.

Tony continued to stare down like a very unhappy house master. Clearly it was my responsibility to fill the void.

'I hope it was OK to use the ... uh ... Jewish hoookaaah?' Considering that my lips had vanished, I was quietly proud of my lucidity.

'Jordanian. The genuine Jordanian hookah.'

'It was incon-gru-ous anyway, mate,' I explained, meaning the hunting print.

Tony waved his letter. 'He won't put a penny into it!'

I reached deep into my memory bag. 'That jade boutique you wanted to start in … uh … Hamburg?'

'Hampstead. The old fart has decided to sink his spare dosh into a project to restore peregrine falcon hunting.'

'So … old mate, you're jaded because …' I started giggling, ' … your bird has flown.'

My host took in Thuy's unbuttoned shirt. 'Piss off, funnyman,' he drawled. Somehow he still sounded urbane.

I remember crawling through a bed of orchids which gave way to the floor of a taxi where a beautiful Burmese girl was tickling me as she unzipped my money belt.

* * *

The road was a ribbon of neon when the highwayman came riding, sliding in his own oil slick down Pattpong Road. He braked on worn drums and straddled the sides of his shuddering Honda 750-4 as he waited for me to slip through the Bangkok crowd. With no helmet, goggles Rommel-style on his forehead and a silk bandana stretched across aristocratic nose, Lord Tony looked magnificent. Unfortunately, his ancient motorbike stalled in the slightest downpour, and in Bangkok, it rains nearly every day. So you only sighted Tony and the Honda on the most balmy and optimistic of evenings.

'Climb aboard, little Australian person,' he ordered. I wrapped my arms around his waist.

'Is this how you liked it at Eton?' I enquired. But Tony was revving the old four-lunger.

'I have a business proposition,' he shouted, as we accelerated towards the Tudor Inn.

'You and Thuy could earn up to five per cent commission, about 60,000 baht,' he revealed, as we sank into the red upholstered seats.

The Tudor Inn is a replica of an English pub, authentic in every detail except for the mini-skirted Thai waitresses who serve tankards of cold Singah beer. 'I don't want you, just Thuy to translate. But you are a pigeon pair these days. How are finances?'

'Not bad.'

'Desperate, I heard.' He smiled. 'You will have a small part to play after Thuy has done her translating. Once I have my goods, it will be your job to watch over them. You do have a sort of ...?' He looked out of the bar window for inspiration and his eyes fell on the Honda. '... working class torque. He who lives outside the law must be honest. Who said that?'

I shrugged.

'Dylan. What album?'

'Blood on the Tracks?'

'John Wesley Harding. Ironic really. Because of your dishonest past, you are obliged to be trustworthy when you deal with people like myself.' Tony was fully briefed on my problems with the law and the prison cell waiting for me in Darwin. 'So, it's agreed? We three will amble off to Chiang Mai.'

'Chiang Mai?'

'Yes, the second biggest city in Thailand, beloved summer retreat of his Royal Highness ...'

'Gateway to the Golden Triangle, beloved opium centre of the bloody world.'

'Michael ... I may smoke the poppy, but I do not traffic in

its derivatives!'

'You know what I'm talking about, Tony! There are at least twenty Drug Enforcement Agency Yanks in Chiang Mai.'

'And you, Michael, are concerned that because of your past indiscretions, you will be listed on their UN financed computers. You're nodding like a metronome again.' I froze. That's a bad habit of mine. Don't even realize I'm doing it.

'You're being paranoid. Why should your petty history interest them? Do you think they'd send one of their expensive Bell helicopters to wrinkle you out of that dense bush across the border?'

'The border! You're not making an illegal crossing into Laos?'

'Never!' Tony waited until I relaxed a little. 'We are making an illegal crossing into old Burma!' He lifted his genuine English tankard to the beams and recited the *Road to Mandalay.* That kind of performance barely raises an eyebrow in the Tudor.

' "…By the old Moulmein pagoda, lookin' lazy at the sea,// There's a Burma girl a' sittin', and I know she thinks of me…" ' 'Your Thuy reminds me of that girl. She has been wasting Christian kisses.' He paused.

' "…On a heathen idol's foot," ' I said, coming in on cue. The only English book in the lounge of my Chinese hotel that hasn't been lifted is the collected works of Kipling.

'Quit with the sour grapes? Why Burma, Tony?'

His Lordship smiled and looked mischievous. 'Two words.'

'Not another of your bloody charades. Just tell me.'

'Two words.'

'A hint, or I walk now.'

He reached up and tapped his finger on a framed Lakes District calendar above our heads.

'Sounds like Tuesday?'

He shot two fingers at me.

'Up yours, too. Oh, second word is Tuesday?'

He nodded and held up a single finger, closed it, screwed up one eye and began to examine it lovingly.

'First word is a gem. Diamond Tue ... OK ... *Ruby Tuesday.* Shit, you're going to smuggle rubies!'

'Shhh! Smuggling is such a melodramatic term. I am merely dispensing with the avaricious middleman.'

'So you'll meet the supplier over the border and you need Thuy to translate?'

'Well deduced, destitute Watson-type person. We depart tomorrow.'

It was drizzling when we left, so I had to help Tony push the Honda onto a taxi truck.

Thuy wanted no part of Lord Tony's deal. She bent her fingers backwards and forwards, almost in synch with my metronome nod, as I tried to sell her on the advantages:

1) Sixty thousand baht was too much to turn down.

2) Tony has reduced the risk.

3) Three Peace Corps types are coming along. What a great cover story! They think they'll be researching a documentary for a student Christian magazine. When Thuy wouldn't budge, I played my blackmail card.

'You want see me in chains at Don Muang Airport?' I mimed a pathetic shuffle. 'Australian Embassy will extradite me. Send me back! Will you wave to me?' She shook her head and burrowed into my chest.

* * *

We caught the night bus to Chiang Mai. Bangkok is carbon monoxide and bazooka taxi exhausts. Most tourists hate it, unless they have sex on the brain. Chiang Mai is mountain air and motor scooter pings, the summer retreat of the old Siam. Most *farangs* love the place. Not me.

As the bus swept across the wide canals, I was remembering another beautiful morning when an old girlfriend with a terrible monkey on her back had cracked a bottle over my sleeping head.

Thuy, however, was acting like a true Thai – living for the day. She wanted to visit her favorite place in her home province before we met the Americans.

'Doi Suthep. We go Wat Doi Suthep Temple!' she insisted, like a kid demanding Disneyland.

So I hired a Yamaha 90 cc and we rode up into the hills above Chiang Mai. Then we mounted the one thousand orange and golden steps that lead to the temple of Doi Suthep. Smiling and puffing, Thuy babbled away about how the sacred elephant carrying the Buddha chose to expire on this mountain peak.

'So the good transport he dies here. They make and they make so this place the most good-looking, most hot place for God in Thailand!'

Willy, my Dutch girlfriend, had loved it too. When Thuy and I walked past the same rows of golden Buddhas I remembered how Willy, following the actions of the Thai faithful, had pressed a matchbox-sized gold leaf onto the stomach of a fat boy. She had been a dedicated follower of too many things.

One thousand metres above sea level the yellow sticking plasters on the cheeks and bellies of the Buddhas were once again fluttering wildly in the breeze.

'Give me few dollars for gold?' Thuy asked and snuggled up against me.

'No way. This lot make too much. They're vampires. You know, like in Buffy. Tonight we should sneak back here and ...' I mimed shaving, 'make these Buddhas skinny. You know, like ... like Paris Hilton.' I didn't say it with a smile, and I didn't get one back.

When we rode home that afternoon, Thuy braced her hands on her knees and wouldn't hold onto me, even on the tight bends.

Being an insensitive bastard that day probably saved my life.

* * *

The Peace Corps lads met us by the old army truck Tony had hired. Lance and Casey said they were engineers and had just arrived in Thailand. They looked to be in their early twenties. With his unlined face and linebacker shoulders, Bill, the reporter and soundman, could have been any age from twenty to thirty. Thuy seemed impressed with the banal observations he was making into the microphone of a pretentiously retro reel-to-reel Nagra recorder. 'This team is ready to go,' Bill reported to the Nagra and just in case whoever he was reporting to was not clear on this point he added that 'the boys are A-OK' and 'going forward, they aim to do good work this fine day.'

'Can't be Californians,' I whispered to Tony.

'Too pale?'

'Yeah, and too eager. Breaches Californian state law to display eagerness.'

'Let's hope they're the trusting Midwestern type,' he muttered out of the side of his mouth before stepping forward and clasping their hands with the enthusiasm of Clinton greeting a crop of new female interns.

The Yanks behaved like good old farm boys. They found it hard to hide their surprise when they learnt my battered face and Thuy's innocent features were an item. I apprised them of this fact as soon as Thuy was out of earshot. My credibility took a dive when she moved past my seat at the tailgate and pointedly sat in the back of the truck next to Bill.

Obviously, she was trying to make me jealous and she was bloody succeeding. I concentrated on keeping my head still as Thuy resumed her intense conversation with Bill about the essence of Buddhism. He was nodding encouragingly as she explained, 'Buddha didn't kick arse like your God. Buddha preached your life, my life, don't mean a goddamn.'

Lance and Casey didn't join in. They had met only the day before and were keen to compare college experiences. Tony was in luck. Our three Christian companions were definitely from the Midwest. I can sleep anywhere, especially if the alternatives are watching your girl friend being drooled over by a God-boy or hearing God-boy's amigos swapping the best lines they could recall from their junior college yearbooks. I woke up a few hours later when we hit some very rough back roads. Tony looked glum.

'What's the matter, mate?' I asked. 'Cat got your opium pipe?' He raised one finger in a way that indicated he was not playing charades.

Bill and Thuy were still intent on their discussion of comparative religions. Lance was extolling the virtues of Rupert, Idaho. 'I can prove it, Case. I've got cold, hard statistical evidence. No good shaking your head. Rupert is *the* potato capital of the U S of A.'

Only the driver knew if we were still in Thailand. Both sides of the largely unguarded Thai-Burma border are virtually identical. All we could see from the truck were steep hills of tropical scrub, which had been slashed and burnt and then terraced to accommodate crops of opium poppies.

Lance was concerned. 'If we're still in Thailand, where the government is fighting a war against opium dealers,' he asked no one in particular, 'how come we're staring at fields of poppies?'

Casey had a solution. 'My guess is that what we're seeing here are the remnants of those crops. The UN has introduced crop substitution programs. They sow stuff like oats.'

Lance seemed satisfied with this explanation.

'You blokes are from farming country, aren't you?' I enquired, in my best Wagga Wagga drawl.

Casey surprised me by anticipating my next move. 'You're wondering why we haven't spotted any oats and barley and the like?' he asked. I shrugged and he carried on. 'Well, from my reading, the UN singles out an area for special attention and they don't move on until it's been won over. My guess is we are travelling past some *un*-substituted fields.'

'Gee, Case,' I said, dropping in a hint of Southern drawl.

'That sounds like the kind of protected hamlet policy they had in Nam.'

Casey carried on in the gentle tone required to communicate with a confused old Paul Hogan who used ancient expressions like Nam. 'We ... I mean the Thais, with assistance from the US and the UN, are fighting poverty and ignorance here. Slash-and-burn agriculture leads to a parasitic existence. From my reading, the local hill tribes around here have quickly appreciated the independence from drug barons that they have enjoyed since the introduction of commercial crop rotation.'

I gave up trying to bait the voice of UNESCO and smiled over at Thuy. No response. She was intently explaining to Bill how women occupy a lower plane of existence. 'Chicks are born to have their arses kicked, it all fixed by Buddha. But that's cool.'

* * *

When I woke again, it was twilight and Tony was opening the tailgate. We were parked next to a row of huts. From a hill high above, little men in black, baggy tops and trousers finished at the knee, were loping towards us. They halted on the lowest terrace and stood looking down, still as ninjas.

'It's their village. Why are they holding back?' Tony wanted to know.

A saying from my short military career clunked inside my head. 'Always take the high ground,' I said. 'Better field of fire.'

Tony waved limply up at the ninjas. A greybeard glided down on short, massive legs and dramatically dropped his

45

hands onto his waistband.

'Zorba!' exclaimed Tony.

I was too absorbed to reply. Something in the folds of Greybeard's waistband had glittered.

In Bangkok, police, security guards, even couriers, strut around with gunslinger holsters. Soldiers twirl machine pistols that resemble giant ray guns. Even small shops are guarded by bellicose Sikhs cradling long-barrelled shotguns. Consequently, when you're standing in the badlands of the Golden Triangle, the home of opium warlords and separatist armies which have been fighting since the Chinese Revolution in 1948, you can become very disturbed about the perverse motivation someone might have for hiding a pistol. I nudged Tony and pointed at the waistband.

'Codpiece?' he suggested. I had to admit the bastard had panache.

Greybeard beckoned us inside the biggest hut. It smelt of mould and pigs and kerosene from the hurricane lamps hanging from the bamboo walls. Our host sat us in a circle and, with the broken-toothed grin of Anthony Quinn playing Mexican bandit, offered us a share of the communal pot. Casey dutifully dipped into the pot. He fished out a greenish lump of chicken, made the mistake of taking a sniff, dropped it, stood up and banged his head on the low rafters. Bill glared at him and turned to Thuy.

'Please thank the headman and tell him that unfortunately all six of us are vegetarians.'

Greybeard ran his eyes contemptuously across our faces as Thuy delivered the message.

I wasn't going to be protected by this wimp of a Yank who

thought he could order around my girlfriend.

'I'm no vegan,' I boomed and winked at Tony. I dipped a spoon into the pot and pulled out a lump of chicken and rancid rice. He saw what I was up to and joined me in a pantomime of joyful chewing. It was easy in the dim lamplight to palm the stuff and drop it onto the earthen floor behind us. The Americans were amazed. Their looks turned to disgust when Tony and I followed local custom by wiping our hands on the back of a young girl who placidly knelt before us for that purpose.

Greybeard became serious and made an earnest speech which Thuy translated. 'The buyers want to check you tonight. Not tomorrow. He will take us there. We shift our arses now or no deal!'

Thuy and Tony went into a huddle with the Yanks. I guessed he was pitching them some yarn about there being no need to bother themselves going over the border so late at night. He certainly didn't want them around while he was bartering for illegal rubies. But Bill stood up and determinedly shouldered the bulky Nagra. An unhappy Tony crawled over to me.

'Wouldn't it be wonderful, Michael, pooped though we are, if we could wrap this whole thing tonight? One hour across the hill, meet the lads with the *you know what*, and then back before dawn for a well-earned visit to the and of nod? What say?'

'*No* is what I say. Look at Thuy, she's stuffed. I'm stuffed.'

'Michael, old mate, you heard the man. It has to be tonight. Do you want to go home empty-handed?'

Under most circumstances, that argument would have

been sufficiently eloquent. But Tony was too insistent. Bill whispered to Thuy. She shifted over to me and slid her arm around my waist, and breathed into my ear like a bar girl in Pattpong.

'*Chi kap*, baby. We hit the sack late. *Mai pen rai kap*. OK, baby?'

Thuy and Bill had become too close. It was better to get this business out of the way. I squeezed her arm and nodded.

As we left the hut, Greybeard produced a bottle of *arak*, the lethal rice wine of Asia, and began passing us little metal cups.

'Tell him we don't drink,' whined Casey.

'That would be very bad-mannered,' I insisted. 'Some of us chicken-fanciers have a reputation to maintain. Right, Tony?' His lordship gave what the classics call a wan smile and reluctantly held out his cup. On a count of three, we downed our *arak* in one synchronized movement.

Tony gasped. 'A skunk carrying a lit blowtorch has just slid down my large intestine.'

I burped and thanked our host. Greybeard chuckled. He raised one of his strangler hands and spilt some *arak* onto the ground. Then he snatched the pistol from his sash. I froze. But not his Lordship; he moved behind me in a dazzling sidestep.

The pistol disappeared behind Greybeard's back. He pulled a lighter from the front of that multi-purpose waistband and laid a flame to the spilt wine. It ignited like a pile of gunpowder. Greybeard grinned and looked us over.

'I believe I'll have another,' I heard myself say.

'Absolutely!' said a shaky voice behind me.

The headman laughed approvingly and patted our backs

as Tony and I raised our cups for nervous seconds.

* * *

In single file, bent forward, about twenty strong, we started up the mountain. No inhibitions now about firearms. The ninjas cradled assault rifles and Greybeard sported one of those Bangkok ray guns. Bill didn't seem worried about the weaponry. He looked down at the village where Lance and Casey had chosen to stay behind and waved his Maglite torch at them – a full-armed, back-and-forth confident wave.

'Reminds me of a painting of yours, Tony,' I told his Lordship.

'Oh?'

'The one of the Cornish wrecker, waving an unsuspecting vessel onto the rocks.'

Tony looked away. I was really scared then. If Tony felt guilty, we were in big trouble.

Bill caught up to us. 'Move your asses!' he ordered, and then ran to help pull my girl up the slope.

'Is that proper Christian talk?' I asked Tony.

One arduous hour later, we halted and watched the ninjas fan off into the scrub. Greybeard conferred with Thuy. She turned to Bill. 'He say he bug out now. He have hassles if he go more far. But his son do number one good guide job.'

I went to speak to Thuy. But Tony nudged me. 'Shut up and keep your head down,' he hissed.

All the ninjas disappeared into the scrub, except for one edgy boy in his teens with 'expendable' virtually glowing on his forehead.

After another hour, we reached the outskirts of a camp. There was no doubt I'd been conned. Ruby smugglers don't need sentries with M16s. Under the dazzle of their own Maglites, they searched us for weapons. Then we were marched through the steel gates of the camp, between rows of bamboo huts and tents up to an army hut.

The guy in charge had the shaven head and psychopathic stare of a young Chiang Kai-shek. He watched impatiently as the guards emptied Tony's pack onto the table and thick bundles of American dollars tumbled out. Tony, all panache stripped away, began babbling to Thuy.

'Tell him this $50,000 is a mere down payment ... uh ... I mean ... a little action to show I'm a straight shooter. Tell the Generalissimo that I hate his Communist enemies and I look forward to scoring much heroin, white powder, from him in his glorious ... solidarity ... uh ... good buddy times to come.'

Bill seemed relaxed, as if he had always been aware of Tony's true plan. Even Thuy was translating as if she had known what to expect.

'He say you very gutsy guy to come here. He think you number one. He say you on your way to being big shot!'

'Thank the General. Tell him the Kuomintang Army of Northern Burma has always been my favourite political cause. I mean, number one, really, and ask him very nicely if I can check out his factory. You know, where he cooks up the heroin, as a sign he's of good faith, you know a regular guy and can deliver in the ... glorious days to come.'

Young Chiang Kai didn't appreciate Tony's request. I could see his side of things. Factories are plastic-roofed smokehouses where the opium is refined into bricks of heroin. They take time to organize, have to be built by a large river, and present camouflage difficulties. He who holds the factories in the Triangle holds the whip hand.

'He say no way. Factory his goddamn business. He sling you heroin. You buy and that all! You goddamn lucky he don't blow you away.' Thuy's voice was shaking as she translated. She looked over at Bill who was casually checking his watch. 'What we do, *adjan?*' she asked.

Bill's solution was to drop into a crouch.

'Tell 'em to freeze!' he yelled. The Nagra console was open. Bill was holding an unpinned grenade in one hand and a flare gun in the other. He stepped back towards the open door, angled the gun and fired a flare into the air.

One of the soldiers aimed at Bill. The crazy freak ignored him and threw the grenade into the centre of the room. There was a huge explosion. I rolled through the door and heard another boom. My ears were ringing. I felt for my back. No shrapnel wounds! No wetness! In the light from the camp generator, I could see purple smoke pouring out of the hut.

Smoke bomb! The Yank had dropped a smoke bomb into the hut. Guards and civilians were running everywhere. The explosions were coming from mortar shells that were hitting the far side of the camp.

Bill and Thuy rushed past me, with Tony following. I sprinted after them. Bill ran through the open gate and confidently headed uphill to where the mortars were firing and led us under their trajectory. You could tell he was young and inexperienced: he was trusting his own artillery.

Tony was badly shocked. Even as he ran, he was spitting out accusations to no one in particular.

'You are a filthy liar. You said this was a recce. You are a filthy liar!'

As we ran towards the mortars, Greybeard charged into view waving his ray gun. A pack of ninjas followed and, in the middle, came two *farangs* in full Rambo gear. Sure enough, these were the Trojan horses of the Midwest: Lance with a field radio and Casey, who was steadying a light mortar. As his team dropped to cover the camp below, Bill passed his Maglite and a map to Tony.

'Go back the way we came,' he ordered. Tony ignored him and kept spitting out complaints. Bill grabbed back the navigation aids and gave them to me.

'When you make the village,' he snapped, 'there'll be a driver waiting. Tell him, *One:* Special Agent Bryant said to take you back to Chiang Mai; and *Two:* we must be re-supplied within twenty-four hours.' Then, so help me, this reincarnation of Indiana Jones took Thuy in his arms and kissed her.

'I'll see you in Bangkok,' promised Indiana.

* * *

I would like to claim that I dragged a squealing Tony along the mountain trail. But as soon as his Lordship realized there was a safe exit, he calmed down and tramped out with dignity. Towards the end of the trek, as we were scrutinizing the map in the early light, he mumbled a type of apology.

'I honestly thought we were just going to set up the show. Do a recce and cheerfully depart. You can't trust these Choir Boy types.'

We made the village by 7 am. Sure enough, Bill had spoken

with a straight tongue. Waiting there was a driver with a truck standing by. But he wouldn't budge until he was paid an additional bribe.

Tony claimed he had no money. I searched him, but nothing had stuck to his fingers. No wonder he was so depressed. After 15 minutes of polite argument, Thuy admitted that Bill had given her money and she paid the driver.

Thuy sat in the cab with the driver. As Tony and I sat in the back, swigging on a canteen of *arak*, his Lordship told me his side of the story

'The DEA approached me. Said I had the appropriate, slightly dubious credentials to convince the wrong people. They've been pressuring the Thais for months to mount a proper raid across the border. Eventually, the Agency got permission for one operation that had to capture a factory and some big fish like the General.'

'Why did you need me? Appropriate, slightly dubious credentials?'

'Don't underrate yourself, Michael; your credentials are very dubious. You helped make me look bad enough for the job. But the Yanks lied. Last night was supposed to be nothing more than a recce.'

'Is that your bloody mantra?'

Tony licked the sticky *arak* from his lips. 'You don't know how lucky you were. You and Thuy were expendable. But ...'

'Bill fell for Thuy.'

Tony tipped up the canteen and sucked as hard as he could before turning back to me.

'I suppose Bill thought he had to look after you. If you'd been wasted, Thuy might have been upset.'

'Might have?' I snapped.

'Dead lovers have a habit of fouling up a new romance.' Tony was probably having a dig at me about Willy. He had always blamed me for what happened to her. Well, he could get in line.

'You should be grateful,' he continued, growing in confidence. 'If I hadn't brought Thuy along, she wouldn't have fallen for Bill and you might not be here now.'

I was too exhausted to respond. I swallowed the last of the *arak* and thought about that Indiana Jones farewell.

'Bill must have spent too many hours in movie theatres in places like Rupert, Idaho. What do you reckon?'

Tony didn't hear me. He was curled up like an angelic choirboy. I steadied my head and looked out with bleeding eyes on the *un*-substituted fields.

Roger Vickery is a Sydney-based teacher, barrister and sometime film-maker. His short stories and poetry, published in Australia and overseas, have won over 40 awards.

Several of his stories are set in Thailand of the late-1970s and 80s – a turbulent period for Thais and *farangs* alike, but a godsend for an aspiring crime writer. Many of the incidents and characters he portrays stem from the author's own experiences while working as a freelance film-maker in the Kingdom.

In fact, Roger's first published story was based on the avuncular host of Pattpong's best jazz bar who, despite being Western Australia's most wanted escapee, enjoyed the enthusiastic patronage of several Australian diplomats. There is more than a little of that character in Lord Tony himself. Roger is currently working on two other stories that deal with the central characters introduced here in 'Lord Tony's Deal'.

Thailand

WET NIGHTMARES

JIM ALGIE

The fat guy grabbed Watermelon's hand, pulled her onto his lap and squeezed her breasts. When he kissed her, she felt like digging her long, sparkly silver fingernails into the soft spot at the bottom of his throat and ripping out his vocal cords – anything to stop him from treating her like she was public property and shoving his tongue down her throat so she almost gagged on the taste of garlic and gin-and-tonic.

Instead, she pulled her mouth away, giggled, and said, 'You pay bar, I come your room, okay?' He shook his head and his bearded jowls flapped.

Pay the fucking bar fine or stop squeezing my tits, she thought.

Watermelon leaned over, kissed him on the cheek, and smiled. In her helium-high voice, she squeaked, 'You handsome man.'

'No, I am fat, ugly man – *ja*.'

She suppressed a laugh; at least he was right about that.

Then she looked over at the stage of the Hot Pussies Go-Go Bar, where nine or ten Thai women were dancing in matching red thongs and bras to a techno song. The flashing lights painted their faces and bodies with shades of pink, blue, orange and green. At the front, Bird was rubbing her crotch against a silver pole and smiling down at some cute young guy sitting at the bar which ringed the stage.

That greedy bitch had stolen Watermelon's customer last night after she'd been sitting with the guy for two hours. It was only halfway through the month and Bird had been bragging to the other girls that she'd already racked up ten bar fines and eighty-five drinks. Although Watermelon, tiny and fair-skinned, considered herself the prettiest girl who worked there, she'd had a dismal month: only two bar fines and fifteen drinks.

As Bird turned around to rub her crack up and down the chrome pole, the German leered at her.

'Don't look she. She have AIDS.' It was the kind of vicious lie Watermelon had been telling lately about any of the girls who made more money than she did, to the point where none of the other go-go dancers wanted anything to do with her.

After four years of working at various go-go bars around Patpong, she couldn't hustle the way she used to. More and more often, when she wasn't dancing, she found herself sitting alone in the corner, thinking of ways she could get enough money to start her own little beauty parlour in Bangkok, bring her daughter back from her parent's village in Chiang Mai province, and find a new husband who had a decent job.

She didn't think that was too much to ask for. So why was she stuck here?

To end up as a whore in this life, she must've committed some terrible sins in her previous one, probably even killed somebody. That's why she was being punished like this. But as long as she kept doing good deeds when she could, and giving alms to Buddhist monks, she might be able to improve her bad karma.

With the money she'd already saved up, all she needed was a couple of thousand more dollars, and then she'd have enough to go into business for herself.

The fat guy beside her, now rubbing her pussy through her thong, was going to be her ticket out of here. Looking at his gold Rolex watch, diamond ring and Versace shirt, it was obvious that he was rich. Since he was staying in a fancy hotel, it was also obvious that his expensive clothes and jewellery weren't the fakes that they sold in the Night Bazaar right outside the bar.

Earlier, when he'd taken out his wallet to give her a tip, she'd noticed that it was stuffed with American dollars. Seeing that, Watermelon lied and said she was going on a trip to Chiang Mai soon – and was it a good idea to take traveller's checks with her?

'I never use them in Thailand. I come here three times every year for ten years now, and I never have some problem. Thailand is very safe, *ja*.'

So maybe he had more money and jewellery back in his hotel room. Maybe there was an expensive camera she could steal, or even a video camera. But would he keep the rest of his cash and valuables in the safe-deposit box?

He'd already given her a one-hundred baht tip and bought her three 'Lady Drinks', so he must like her. Now she had to get him to pay the bar fine and take her back to his hotel. Hot Pussies was going to close in half an hour, and she was worried that he might wander off to an after-hours disco and pick up someone else. After another song, she'd have to go back onstage to dance again. Her feet were already sore from shuffling and grinding all night in her high heels, and if she did go back onstage, then Bird or one of the other girls might steal her customer. She couldn't take that chance. She had to get him to pay the bar fine now.

With one hand, Watermelon stroked the lump in his trousers, while she rubbed his right nipple through the silk shirt. His blue eyes closed slightly. She then put her hand inside his shirt and circled the nipple with her fingernail as the lump in his trousers grew. The man's eyes closed a little more and she could feel his heart pumping out of sync with the pounding drums.

Squeezing the lump reminded her of milking cows on the family farm. She opened another button, leaned over and rimmed the nipple with her tongue before taking it between her teeth and sucking on it.

His eyes were closed now, and the lump was wriggling as she put her tongue in his ear and tasted some bitter wax. Then Watermelon moaned, 'I so horny. You pay bar for me, okay?'

His eyes opened and there was a dazed smile on his face, like he was awakening from a very pleasant dream. '*Ja*, I pay bar.'

Watermelon smiled, gave him a hug and kissed his prickly cheek. 'Tank you.'

In the dressing room, she changed into a bright pink mini-dress with matching high heels and took all of the perfume, makeup, underwear, tampons, her miniature panda bear, and the capsules she was going to use to drug him out of her locker, and put them in her Snoopy backpack. In the cracked mirror, she wiped the lipstick smears off her cheeks and chin with a wad of damp toilet paper, put on some fresh lipstick, and then brushed her long, lustrous black hair.

Walking out of the bar behind the fat guy, she stopped near the front of the stage and called out Bird's name. When the other woman turned around, Watermelon gave her the finger, yelled, 'Fuck off!' and giggled. As she did it, she imagined that it wasn't only the greedy bitch she was telling to fuck off: it was also every customer in the bar, the owner, the *mamasan*, and the entire red-light district of Patpong.

* * *

In the back of the taxi with her customer, Watermelon's guilt and nervousness about robbing him gave her an upset stomach. But how many men had ripped her off? Even after she'd told them in the bar, or in another after-hours club, that her prices were fixed for 'short-time' and 'all-night', they still kept cheating her. The younger, better-looking guys were usually the worst: they never wanted to pay or they lied and said they would.

As she looked out the window of the taxi at a little stand selling red-pork-and-egg-noodles soup, she remembered that one cute guy with the spiky blond hair. Among her customers – the manicured bankers and cologne-reeking diplomats, the alcoholic whoremongers and the tattooed backpackers like him – many shared the same fantasy: They were such virile lovers they could even make a prostitute come.

Watermelon spurred on his fantasy with a series of sighs, cresting on each breath as she moaned, 'Oh yeah...oh yeah. You hit my G-spot,' like an actress repeating lines in a play she'd performed dozens of times, all the while wondering what she would eat afterwards. The sweet green curry or the rice noodles with fish balls? And which pair of flats would go with the new top she'd bought that day?

In the throes of arousal, men became such mindless animals that they did not realize she was only engaging them with her body. Her thoughts ranged freely. So it was a little better than working as a seamstress in that garment factory, following patterns on an industrial-sized sewing machine amidst a racket that made the fillings in her teeth ache and nullified all thoughts. That job demanded both her body and her mind, and it didn't pay nearly as well as working in a bar.

Humping away with short, sharp, repetitive strokes, not even varying the tempo at all, he reminded her of the two bunnies she'd bought for her daughter when they got into mating mode.

'Rabbit' was too young and vain to possibly be a good lover. He was more interested in admiring his tattoos, piercings and muscles in the mirror beside the heart-shaped bed than he was in pleasing her, the kind of customer she had often overheard boasting to his friends, 'I shagged that tart rotten last night.' Since few of the men spoke much Thai, they were unaware that the bargirls were constantly ridiculing them. Watermelon repeated his boast about her to Bird, who was sitting in a man's lap beside the bar. Over top of the throbbing dance music, Bird yelled back, 'So you had a really big romance last night?'

Watermelon shouted, 'Are you kidding? It was the most well-paid two minutes of my life.' She and Bird shrieked with laughter.

Another bargirl chimed in with a Thai expression for a premature ejaculator, 'He's a sparrow dipping his beak,' and that set off another chorus of giggles.

All the jokes they made about their customers were less about revenge than a need to prove they were more than just an empty mortar to be pounded by a series of blood-engorged pestles. Any man could rent Watermelon's body. None would ever possess her mind or heart.

But the longer she worked in a bar, the less true that resolution had become.

After she took a shower and put on her clothes, she politely asked him for her money.

'I don't pay for it, luv,' said Rabbit with a sneer.

'You say me already you will to pay, *na*.'

And then there was that smug little smirk of his, like he was so superior to her (she wished she could travel back in time now and return the smirk), followed by 'Nobody likes a whore, dear.' Without even letting her pick up her purse, he grabbed her arm, dragged her out of his hotel room, and slammed the door. For a few minutes she pounded on that door and yelled at him to give back her purse until a security guard came up and said the man had accused her of trying to steal his watch, so he had to throw her out of his room.

After a long argument with the guard, who also knocked on the door repeatedly, the 'cheap Charlie' opened it just wide enough to throw her red purse, emblazoned with gold hearts, on the floor, causing half of the contents to spill out.

Blushing with embarrassment, she quickly shoved the package of condoms and the thong back inside it, then checked her wallet to find that the guy had stolen a thousand baht from her. Not only that, the security guard demanded some money – leaving her with barely enough for cab fare – or, he said, he'd report her to the police for stealing from one of the hotel's guests.

Even that was far from her worst experience though. She forced herself to remember the most terrible encounter because it alleviated her guilt about what she was going to do tonight.

Watermelon couldn't remember if that businessman had been from Japan, or Hong Kong, or Singapore – what did it matter? – but he came into the bar after playing a round of golf and still had his bag and clubs with him.

His sick fantasy was for her to sit on the floor of the 'short-time' hotel with her back against the bed, then spread her legs and sex apart so he could use his putter to try and tap a golf ball inside her. But he was far too drunk to realize it was impossible. After about thirty attempts, he shoved the ball inside her with his fist, raised the club and his other arm above his head, cheered and yelled, 'A hole in one!'

Later, he made her kneel on the bed like a dog while he shoved the thin end of two clubs into her anus and vagina, screwing her with them while masturbating. Naked except for his blue socks and white golf cap, the sadist kept ordering her to look in the big mirror on the wall.

'Look! Look in mirror!'

It wasn't enough for him to make her lose face like this, she thought. *His real excitement depended on Watermelon seeing her shame and his superiority.*

In between gasps and stabs of pain, she continued to look down at the pillow and think *I'm being used as a scapegoat for every woman who's ever rejected this fucking creep. And who wouldn't?*

Because he had a pug-nose like a Pekinese, she decided this client's nickname would be 'Dog'. So when he growled 'You like? You like?', she replied in Thai, 'I'll bet you were born in the Year of the Dog, weren't you?' and giggled.

A hyperactive chatterbox who never knew when to keep her mouth shut – which was the main reason she had so few regular customers – Watermelon kept making jokes he couldn't understand, followed by giggling.

When his pants and moans became whimpers, he grabbed her by the hair, twisted her head around, and shot gobs of disgusting semen all over her face.

Still panting, Dog said, 'You don't laugh at me. Too many women do like this already.'

Then he punched her in the face and broke her nose.

She curled up in a fetal position, wiping the blood, semen and tears from her face with a sheet, while he got dressed, shoved a couple of bills into her pussy, and left without saying a word.

Since that shameful evening six months ago, she'd had trouble looking at her face in the mirror without sneering and telling her reflection: 'You're nothing but a stupid, rotten whore. No decent man is ever going to fall in love with you again and want to marry you because you're so disgusting.'

Until tonight, Watermelon had never stolen much from her clients except for some loose bills, a couple of expensive watches, and a few hundred multi-hued lighters. Since she didn't smoke, she super-glued them, in the shape of peacocks, flowers and elephants, to cover the cracks in the walls of the one-room apartment she shared with three other bargirls.

But she'd been fucked over too many times; now it was her turn to get even and get out of the business. Besides, this fat and hairy guy – Gorilla, as she had dubbed him – was rich, so he wouldn't really miss the money and jewellery anyway, and maybe she'd give him a good blow-job first, so he wouldn't feel too cheated when he woke up.

If he woke up.

She'd heard a couple of stories about prostitutes drugging their clients. The men overdosed and the women ended up going to jail for twenty-five or thirty years. Watermelon knew one of those women and had gone to visit her a few times at a horrible prison in Bangkok. She always brought her some food, cigarettes, tampons or medicine and fashion magazines. She knew these were, in part, selfish gestures: good deeds to help erase her bad karma.

But even working in a go-go bar had to be heaven compared to being imprisoned in a Thai jail, where the cells were so overcrowded that the prisoners had to take turns sleeping on the floor, and the daily food rations consisted of a small bowl of watery rice, and maybe – if you were lucky – a fish head.

Maybe she shouldn't drug this guy. He'd been quite

generous so far and would probably pay her well for sleeping with him tonight.

Then she remembered 'Dog' growling at her 'Look! Look in mirror! You like? You like?' ... and that smirking guy with the blond hair throwing her favourite purse on the floor in the hallway.

What if Gorilla was a sadist, too? What if he stole her money and beat her up, or gave her AIDS, or even killed her?

To reassure herself, she felt around in her backpack for the switchblade she carried and stroked the plastic handle.

Then she looked down and saw Gorilla caressing her bare thigh. How long had he been touching her like that? Why couldn't she feel it?

When she thought about it, over the last four years Watermelon had been groped, kneaded, kissed, licked, bitten, screwed and sodomized so many times that she knew her body was slowly dying and that her heart must look like a withered old rose, turning blacker and getting smaller by the night. If she didn't get out soon, her body and heart were going to die completely. Or she'd end up knifing one of her customers.

But she also had to quit for the sake of her daughter. A couple of weeks ago, she'd telephoned her parent's house in northern Thailand and her five-year-old had picked up the phone. Listening to Duck babble away in that bright voice of hers – a memory of the heart-shaped wind chimes hanging down from the eaves of a Buddhist temple passed through Watermelon's mind –always made her smile and feel like such a proud mother.

It was funny how Duck couldn't pronounce some of the Thai tones properly, so when she wanted to say 'We're a very big family', it sounded like 'We're a very big strawberry'. She explained the mistake to Duck, and they both laughed. In the hope of inspiring her daughter to be more diligent about studying than she'd been, Watermelon taught her the correct tones for 'family' and then made her repeat them a few times until she got them right.

Only about three minutes into their conversation, however, her daughter suddenly asked, 'Mom, are you really a prostitute? Is that why you never come home and visit me?' At first, Watermelon was too stunned to say anything. Then she exploded. 'I never taught you that dirty word, and I don't want to ever hear you use it again! Do you understand? I'm a beautician and I have to work in Bangkok to help support you and my parents, younger sisters, and my two lazy brothers who never do anything but get drunk.'

Duck began crying. Watermelon rubbed her forehead while scolding herself for being such a bad mother and a liar.

Just then, the taxi pulled up in front of the Watergate Hotel.

* * *

Watermelon took a hot shower and thought about her plan. Another go-go dancer had told her that the best way to drug a client was to rub some sedatives into her breasts and nipples. But wouldn't he be able to taste the drug when he licked her boobs? Seeing how drunk and horny he was, maybe not.

How many capsules should she use? One? Two? Since the guy was so fat, maybe she should use all three. But would that kill him? (The pharmacist had told her that five of them would knock out a tiger.)

Finally, she decided on two capsules, one for each breast.

Before she rubbed the tranquilizers into them, Watermelon moved her gold necklace around so that the tiny Buddha image was facing her back, like she always did before having sex with a customer. That way, the amulet would still protect her, but the Buddha wouldn't be able to see what she was doing.

For lubrication, she put a few globs of Vaseline inside her sex. Then she wrapped a dry towel around herself like a sarong and walked into the cool, air-conditioned room. At the foot of the bed, she put her backpack on the floor with the switchblade under it.

Gorilla was lying on top of the covers, holding the remote in his hand and channel surfing with the volume turned down. Except for the little lamp with the white shade beside the bed and the flickering shadows cast by the TV, the huge room was dark.

She lay down beside him, smiled and giggled. 'How are you, honey?'

He kept staring at the TV. 'Drunk and lonely.'

'Why lonely? I am here, *na*.'

'*Ja*, you are here for money, but you don't like me. It's okay. I also don't like me.'

'I like you.'

'*Quatsch*! Don't speak bullshit! I don't like people speaking bullshit.'

What was he so angry about? Was it just all the gin?

Then it occurred to her that the tranquilizers might be seeping into her bloodstream and she'd be the one who fell asleep or overdosed. If she had murdered someone in a previous life, maybe it was this guy and he was here to get revenge? Drugging herself to death while he watched – now that would be fitting karma.

While Gorilla went on and on about how much he missed, and still loved, his ex-wife Karla, she looked around the dark room. Over by the balcony were two suitcases, but she couldn't see any cameras or jewellery lying around. So maybe they were in the wardrobe? Or was there a safe in the room?

Sitting on the edge of the bed, pretending to listen, she tried to stroke his hand, but he pushed it away.

Now he told her about his job, working as a medic at a clinic for Burmese refugees along the border and gave her a long lecture about Burmese politics and why she should never go there, because tourist dollars helped to support their military regime.

With only two days off a month, how was she supposed to go anywhere, except if a customer took her on vacation and paid the bar? And who would ever want to visit some poor, boring country like Burma? The only places she wanted to visit were Singapore, for shopping; Hong Kong, because they had a Disneyland; and America, because everyone looked so rich and beautiful in the TV shows she watched.

Watermelon switched off the lamp and squeaked in her helium-high voice, 'You tink too much. Don't worry, be happy.'

He stroked her hair. '*Ja*, and you think not enough.' For the first time that night, he laughed.

With her on top, they began kissing. Gorilla pulled the towel up over her ass, cupped her buttocks in his palms and kneaded them. His beard scratched her face. Raising herself up on one hand, Watermelon pulled the towel down over her small breasts so that he could lick them.

As he sucked her nipples, greedy as an infant for milk and for love, she felt a surprising affection for him that was maternal, not sexual, because he seemed so helpless and needy. The feeling only lasted for a few seconds – until he bit her nipple and made her wince – but it was still good to know that she could feel something for a man besides anger and bitterness.

The pain evaporated while nervousness crept into her mind. He was really licking and kissing her breasts all over, ensuring that he'd get the full dosage. Would it be enough to kill him? How long would it take before he fell asleep?

He rolled her off of him and kissed her neck while he pushed one … and two … and then three fingers inside her. But since that night with the golfer, she'd felt nothing when they penetrated her down there but a series of chills that slithered up from between her legs and settled in her stomach, like when a gynaecologist put a cold, metal speculum inside her.

Worried that her body, and Gorilla, were both dying on her, she resorted to one of the tricks she used when sleeping with a really ugly customer: rerunning erotic fantasies from her adolescence. Closing her eyes, Watermelon pretended that it was Johnny Superstar fingering her. She saw the pop singer's effeminate face appear in her mind and silently asked him: 'Why do all the men that I'm most attracted to always turn out to be gay?'

Johnny, smiling, said, 'I used to be gay, my lovely sweetheart, but you turned me into a normal man and now I want to marry you. I'd also love for us to have a child together and –'

Gorilla crushed that fantasy by climbing on top of her, burying Watermelon under his prickly bulk after she'd only felt a few pangs of heartburn for her lost and silly dreams of teenage love. Automatically, she moaned and sighed with false passion when she only felt sweaty and claustrophobic. But Gorilla was not like her more aggressive customers who wielded their cocks like killers armed with knives, stabbing her with violence and vengefulness. The German knew that he was too big for her and slowed down. He whispered in her ear, 'You are like a fine piece of china, the most beautiful girl I ever have touched. I don't want to hurt you in some way.' She wished he hadn't said that because, for the first time that night, he became a real person to her; not a customer, not an animal, but a human being. The drug, combined with all the gin, must have been really kicking in now, because Wilhelm's voice took on a new undercurrent of softness.

'Karla, do you love me still?' Some of her customers had requested a 'girlfriend experience', but no one had ever asked her to play their ex-wife before.

Acutely aware of the sweat pooling in her stomach and needling at the corners of her closed eyes, Watermelon hesitated. She had not been hard-wired to provide any automatic responses to a request like this. Half-heartedly, she said, 'Sure, baby, I always love you.'

His sweat, salty as tears, dripped on to her closed lips and eyelids, impregnating her with his sadness. 'You will never leave me again, will you?'

Not daring to open her eyes, but with a little more sympathy, she cooed, 'No, never. I always stay with you.'

Reassured, he began moving his hips again, but slower, more gently, like a man making love to his wife, seeking an intimacy and a connection above and beyond the merely physical. His consideration penetrated a deeper part of her that few of her customers had ever accessed before. Vignettes from her marriage, beginning at the age of sixteen, to a southern Thai Muslim and livestock trader, flickered across her mind like scenes from a grainy film shown at a Buddhist temple fair. Resplendent in his white fez and striped sarong, Hasan smoked tobacco wrapped in a *nipa* palm leaf. Each time he spilled an ash, he licked the tip of his index finger, picked it up and put it in the ashtray. It was a small gesture which had grown larger in time because she'd never seen anyone else do that and probably never would again.

It also said a lot about how neat, gentle, and meticulous he was. Unlike her previous boyfriends, he did not expect her to clean up after him, not even a single cigarette ash. After his daily reading of the Quran, her darkly handsome husband always kissed the cover of the book before putting it back on the shelf. Then he would teach her another expression in Arabic that made both of them laugh.

'Trust in Allah, but keep your camel tied up.' He also enjoyed teasing her about the more extreme elements of Islam that he did not believe in. 'You know, sweetheart, by law I could have four wives, but since you're like ten different women rolled into one, I've already got about eight more than I can handle.'

Watermelon sat down on his lap and tweaked his nose. 'If you even have one other wife, I'll cut your dick off with a machete and feed it to the pigs.' It was the most offensive thing she could possibly say to a Muslim man, but instead of taking offence, he laughed; his long, feminine eyelashes, which she thought were his most attractive feature, fluttered as he laughed.

'Oh, you're such a country girl with all your passion, intensity, and terrible manners. You've got more spirit than all of those prissy, boring office ladies in Bangkok and Had Yai put together.'

Eighteen months after the wedding, Watermelon answered a phone call from his brother informing her that Hasan, barely twenty, had been killed in a motorcycle accident while visiting his family down south. According to Muslim tradition, they had to bury the body within 24 hours of death. She would not have the chance to see him one final time or attend his funeral.

That, more than anything else, had continued to haunt her. How could she have ever explained to him that she'd slept with hundreds of men, but only ever made love to him? And that grief can don many disguises indistinguishable from madness and not-giving-a-damn depravity.

Watermelon was making love to Hasan. Wilhelm was making love to Karla. How could two people performing the most intimate of acts be so completely lost to each other? This was not sex so much as a form of psychotherapy and mutual grieving. In that, it was preferable to grieving alone.

The ghost of her husband, now inhabiting this man's body, pushed his way deeper into her, conjuring a recurring nightmare ...

At opposite ends of a bridge made from the stretched umbilical cord of their daughter stood Watermelon and

Hasan. They called out to each other, but the wind whipped their words away. Holding on to the ropes on each side, Watermelon walked towards her husband, foot over foot, on a swaying ribbon of flesh as slender as a tightrope. Hasan walked towards her. But the more they walked, the farther away from each other they got.

The wind hurled dead owls and palm leaves at her. Digging grit out of one eye, Watermelon watched as the wind grew arms that picked him up and threw him over the ropes. Limbs flailing, he plummeted into a black pit. She let out an ear-piercing scream.

Thinking, perhaps, that she was having an orgasm, Wilhelm quickened his pace and, with their thighs slapping together, they filled each other with the desolation of their lovelorn lives, boiled down into the most primitive elements of bodily secretions and saltwater tears.

Wilhelm lay down beside her, panting heavily and groaning. 'You okay?' she asked.

He put his hand on his heart. Ghostly, blue-white images from the TV flickered across his sweaty face. 'I have terrible pain here,' he said and patted his heart. 'Maybe I am having a heart attack.'

Watermelon swallowed noisily, and it sounded to her like an admission of guilt. When she looked over at him, his eyes were closed and he wasn't moving. She tried to wake him up, but couldn't. Oh no! Watermelon grabbed his wrist and felt his pulse beating. But for how much longer?

What should she do? She wasn't a murderess. She didn't want him to die. So maybe she should call security and make up some bullshit story; they wouldn't know she'd drugged him.

Chewing on her long, sparkly silver fingernails, Watermelon thought about her daughter ('Mom, are you really a prostitute?'), and then Dog and his golf clubs ('Look in mirror!').

No, she had to stop being a whore. She had to do it for Duck.

Quickly, she got dressed and turned on the lamp beside the bed. Gorilla was snoring. Good.

Watermelon crept over to the two suitcases by the balcony, opened the big one and riffled through the contents: shirts, jeans, socks and underwear. Then she opened the smaller suitcase and ... hit the jackpot! It was full of plastic bags containing gold Rolex watches, diamonds, rubies, and sapphires. But her smile went flat when she realized they were probably fakes. Either that or this guy was a robber, too.

Stealing from a thief?

'*Wen gum* [That's karma],' she muttered.

Suddenly, a hand grabbed her by the hair and pulled her head back until it felt like her neck was going to snap. Looking up, she saw a dark beer belly.

'You stupid bitch,' he said in a groggy voice. 'You think you fool me with this drugging trick? No, I fool you.'

Gorilla tried to pull her to her feet, but only tore out a clump of Watermelon's hair. Her scalp on fire, she scurried across the floor on all fours to grab her Snoopy backpack and groped for the switchblade, only to hear it click open behind her. 'I have your knife,' he said.

Watermelon ran for the door in the dark hallway. Feeling around on the carpet for her high heels, she grabbed one of them and stood up to see the silhouette of a monster lumbering towards her. With her fingers wrapped around the toe of the shoe, she pulled it back over her shoulder, took a step forward, and smacked him in the face with the sharp stiletto heel.

'*Scheiße*!'

Watermelon dropped the shoe and tried to whip the door open, but it banged against the chain. Just as she slid the chain off and opened the door, Gorilla flicked on the light in the hallway. The sudden flash blinded her. She blinked rapidly and looked over her shoulder. Standing there naked, he stared at her with tears seeping from one blue eye and blood weeping from an empty socket. His other eye stared at her from the palm of his hand.

Feeling as stunned as he looked, she stood there, muttering, 'I'm sorry, I'm sorry ...'

Watermelon then ran down the hallway and slammed the button for the elevator.

One of them was on floor 18, the other on 12.

'Hurry up! Hurry up!'

Down the hallway she saw Gorilla, a towel around his waist, lumber out of the room and bellow, 'Wake up, everybody! Wake up! There is a thief in our hotel!' Watermelon bolted for the stairway.

Holding the metal railing to propel herself around the corners, her bare feet slapped against the concrete stairs while the numbers of the floors flashed by: 6, 5, 4, 2 ...

Out of breath, she stopped on the ground floor, her heart drumming against her breast. What if he had caught the elevator and was waiting for her in the lobby with one blue eye in his hand? What if he'd called Security? But she couldn't stay here, and waiting would only increase the chance of her getting caught.

Wiping the sweat from her forehead, she walked across the cool marble floor of the gleaming lobby, feeling very suspicious in her bare feet. Fortunately, nobody seemed to be around except for the doorman and the front desk clerk.

She smiled and politely asked the desk clerk for her ID card; it was a fake, so it didn't matter if he'd written down the name and number. For once, she was grateful for the condescending way he dropped her ID on the counter without so much as a word or even a glance.

Quickly, she strode towards the front door, shooting glances over her shoulder at the blinking numbers of an elevator descending (6 ... 5). Up ahead was the doorman, who stared at her bare feet and frowned. (4 ... 3). The doorman was dressed in this old-fashioned Siamese costume of bright silk. Earlier, when she'd walked in with her customer, he'd opened the door for them, but he made no effort to do so now. She heard the ring of the elevator behind her, indicating it had reached the lobby.

Just as she put her hand on the door, she looked around to see a young white guy walk out of the elevator. Watermelon exhaled audibly and smiled.

When the taxi was six streets away from the hotel and she hadn't seen any police pick-up trucks or motorcycles, she figured she was in the clear.

It was sickening though to remember how she'd knocked Gorilla's eye out with her high heel. If she didn't make a decent donation to the temple in her village, the Buddha was going to be very, very angry with her.

After she'd visited her daughter and family for a couple of

months – Gorilla and the police would've given up looking for her by then – Watermelon knew she'd have to come back to Bangkok to work in another bar. Since her parents could only afford to send her to school for six years, she didn't have many other choices. Obviously, she couldn't go back to Patpong; but some of her roommates worked at a new go-go bar called Wild Women in Nana Plaza, so maybe she'd work there and finally meet some rich guy who wanted to marry her.

Watermelon let out a yawn that made her lower jaw tremble and slumped down in the back seat. She could still feel Wilhelm's bulk (or was it all the guilt and disappointment?) pushing down on her chest, along with the dead weight of every customer she'd slept with over the past four years. How many had it been? Two hundred? Three hundred? As many as four hundred? She wasn't sure, but it felt as if she had that invisible Siamese ghoul who sits on the stomachs of dreamers while they sleep and slowly suffocates them to death sitting on her own chest right now.

If she kept saving her money, however, and stayed away from drugs and gambling like she'd done so far, then maybe in another year or two she'd be able to set up her own little beauty parlour and bring her daughter to live with her in Bangkok.

Whatever happened, Watermelon swore to herself and made a promise to Hasan's spirit, that Duck would never end up as a prostitute.

When the taxi stopped at a red light, the driver looked back at her and sharked a grin that made Watermelon shiver and look away. Using a slang term for a one-night stand, he said, 'Do you want to go up to heaven? I have a big rocket that'll take us there in a very short time.' Even though the driver was at least fifty, he laughed and laughed like a teenager.

Resigned to her bad karma for the next few years, but none too happy about it, Watermelon pushed herself up in the backseat with her elbows and smirked at him in the rearview mirror like Rabbit had once done to her.

'How much are you willing to pay, *Mr Rocket*? So you can go up to heaven and I can go down to hell.'

Jim Algie has worked as a security guard in an insane asylum, a gravedigger, a journalist, and a nomadic punk rock musician – an appropriate apprenticeship for practicing the black arts of *weirdsmithing*. His most recent books include *Bizarre Thailand: Tales of Crime, Sex and Black Magic*, the guidebook *Travel Pack Thailand* and an upcoming short fiction collection, *The Phantom Lover and Other Twisted Tales from Thailand*. Under its original title, 'Fucked Over', this remade version of 'Wet Nightmares', is one of the prize-snagging stories collected in the latter book, along with 'The Death Kiss of the King Cobra Show' which appeared in *Extremes 2: Fantasy and Horror from the Ends of the Earth*, a volume which won the Bram Stoker award for the best anthology in 2001.

His journalism features have appeared in the *International Herald Tribune*, *CNN Travel.com*, and the *Japan Times*. More importantly, among his favourite musical artists are The Ramones, The Replacements, Leonard Cohen, Cat Power and Ella Fitzgerald.

More jolts, dollops and pixels of wonderful weirdness are available at *http://bizarrethailand.com*.

Singapore

NOVEMBER RAIN

D. BISWAS

Believe me when I tell you I'm a good man, with a sound explanation for the large Louis Vuitton handbag sitting at the back compartment of my wardrobe, though I'm neither married nor live with a woman. The contents of the bag are not your everyday items either ... but more about that later.

A bag like that would tell you that we Singaporeans value our place in society above all else. When we encounter one another for the first time, we behave much like our pet dogs, who sniff each other out during their walks – we check out handbags and shoes and watches to size up our counterparts. So, let me begin by telling you I used to work as a private investigator; if not *for* the law, then by its side. My job gave me the ride of a lifetime, but ultimately washed me up on the shore minus a couple of body parts.

The last guy I chased ended with him getting caught, but I fell onto the MRT tracks at Bishan, and an oncoming train sawed off my legs. I can still feel my shins and feet– they itch and scratch sometimes. But my legs end at my thighs, and I've learned to accept that.

It didn't go as badly as it could have gone. My company retained me as a freelance online investigator, and I still had this large airy apartment. They needed someone with experience to track suspicious activities online.

The automatic wheelchair made life easier, and the leftover tools of my trade provided the only worthwhile entertainment: I often trained my best telescopes and binoculars on my neighbours in the low-cost HDB complex opposite.

I had grown used to snooping on people throughout my career: cheating spouses, company employees, and aggressive loan sharks. I ferreted out their secrets, or pulled the plug on their double lives. Now that I lived alone, looking into other people's lives became my only way of connecting with them. The constant fear of discovery gave me an adrenalin rush – a pale shadow of my bygone days on the job, but a legless man takes what he can get.

One November evening, I saw two young women move in to one of the HDB apartments across the street. They hadn't had time to buy curtains, and I had a clear view of their rooms through window grills. I had my telescopes set beside my black leather couch in my living room: the larger one for greater distances, and the smaller one for nearer objects, which I concealed behind dark-grey blinds. As usual, I tried to lip-read, guess the relationship between the women, their nationalities. I wanted to know their covert, veiled lives. I pegged the girls down as Filipinas come to Singapore in search of work. One wore a black uniform, and I knew straight-off she worked at the reception of a hotel. The other wore jeans and a top, and going by her bulky arms, held a job that involved physical labour. She looked too self-assured to be a maid, and her steady walk intrigued me. It gave her grace and authority at the same time.

That evening, I watched them as they stepped out of their kitchen into the living room. They carried *tapau* packs of food and ate them sitting on the ramshackle sofa by the flickering light of the television. The 'hotel receptionist' went to bed early. The other one, my favourite, stayed up watching TV. Her legs moved from side to side, making her long, loose culottes flutter. Her feet sat on a small wooden table.

As I watched her, I tried to imagine where she worked. Not any place fancy, but not too shabby either. I imagined swinging by her workplace and flirting with her as she went about her business. I may not have legs, but my chest and arms are muscled from lifting the weight of my body onto the wheelchair and off it again.

I could not see what she was watching, because the TV sat on the other side of the window, but it didn't make her happy. She sniffed from time to time, her nose rising, and pursed her lips. Her long hair, possibly wet from washing, lay over her shoulder and she ran her hand through it, untangling it and twisting the hair that came away into a ball. Her spaghetti top pasted to her with sweat. From time to time, she raised the top from her body and blew down her front. I wondered if they had air-conditioning.

Watching this girl was better than calling up people or

throwing parties. Neither would allow me to watch a girl this way. It was better than paying for company, which would have slapped my desperation in my face, and saddled me with a painted mask of fake smiles and sympathy. This flesh-and-blood girl felt as if she were sitting beside me. True, I could not touch her, but one can't have everything.

Near midnight, she got up and pulled off her top. She wore no bra, so her breasts spilled out. They sagged a little on her petite frame, the nipples pointing sideways. My palm sweated, making the telescope's focus-ring slip. The image blurred because I turned the ring the wrong way in my frenzy, and by the time I readjusted it, she had switched off the light in the living room. I waited for her to switch on the light in her room, but she went to bed in the dark.

*　*　*

The next morning, I got my coffee and sat down by the window. It rained in a steady drizzle, and I waited for the girls to wake up. I had finished most of my work the evening before, which left me free to blast old Guns N' Roses songs via iTunes on my surround-sound speakers.

I focused the telescope on the window of the night before, and there she stood. Home alone, she strutted around the apartment like a figure from porn *anime* cartoons: heart-shaped, childlike face unaware of her near-naked body. She wore a pair of pale blue cotton panties and held a pen and notepad, possibly planning furnishings. They certainly needed some curtains. I hoped they wouldn't get them any time soon. Her straight silky hair fell over her hips, and touched her bare thighs. She made notes on the pad, took measurements, and stood chewing her pen, looking at one corner or the other.

She must have been used to walking around without much on, because she still acted as if she had clothes on. It continued to rain as I watched her, the falling drops of water like string curtains. I gripped my telescope with both hands, longing for her to face the window again, as Slash made love to his guitar, playing *November Rain*. I loved that song; the strings made me happy and sad at the same time – calm, centred. They worked this time as well, though she did not return to the window.

That weekend, they put up their curtains. But my girl didn't seem to think she needed them and left them wide open. She and the other girl worked shifts. The star attraction of my telescope worked the day shift and spent most of her evenings at home alone. As if in answer to my prayers, she padded about near-naked and threw off her clothes the minute she came back home from work or wherever.

Once I had figured out her routine, I planned my week's work around her schedule. In the evenings, she went into the living room in a white towel after her shower, wet hair pasted to her body. I resented that towel, she could have used it to dry her hair instead. She sipped from takeaway cups and sometimes walked right to the window.

Later, she sat eating in front of the evening soap on television. I still couldn't see what she watched, but it made her cry a lot. She went to bed by eleven.

* * *

One evening, a month later, I watched my Filipina walking

around as usual in her towel. She turned away from the window and I lost her for a few minutes. I waited for her to come back, nose glued to my telescope. She returned with a tall man, a wiry, tanned *ang moh* who would have made a good race-jockey if not for his height. He wrapped one arm around her neck as they kissed. Her towel slipped down. My hands went to my boxers at the sight and went to work.

The couple went to work as well. The man's T-shirt and shorts flew off as he stumbled and fell back on the sofa, his spidery hands on her breasts. The window cut off my view as she sat on him, her head thrown back. She rose and fell while the dimple on her chin drove me crazy as it went up and down.

As she panted, his hands crept up to her throat, and gripped it hard. Horrified, I held my breath. But she did not struggle, just kept moving faster, her eyes large, frantic. I pulled up my shorts, and began counting the floors to the apartment, wavering between making an emergency call or trying to rush down myself. But before I could grab the phone, the man let go, and she looked up to meet my eyes.

I ducked immediately, and when I got up, she had the towel wrapped around her hair in a turban as she rode piggy-back on the shoulders of her guy, laughing. Her body looked like a violin, her legs out of eyesight, wrapped around his front.

In the weeks that followed, I saw her and the *ang moh* every weekend. They spent most of their time in her room with the curtains drawn. He looked familiar, but I couldn't place him. This bothered me. My whole career had once hinged on remembering faces, but I'd fallen into the habit of never trying to meet people's eyes ever since the wheelchair. I felt like snuffing them out if they turned away first. But losing touch with your skills couldn't be a good thing either.

A week later, on a bright Tuesday, my doorbell rang. My housekeeper only came on Saturdays, and I never had any visitors. The guards hadn't called from the gate to announce a visitor either. When I opened the door, I expected a cleaner, or a courier delivery. But instead, there she stood, my Filipina.

'I can't stand outside, let me in,' she said. 'I saw something shining on your window that day. My boyfriend lives in an apartment on this floor, so I knew exactly where you were.' No preamble, no hello.

She talked as she walked: confident, unselfconscious.

'You don't look too bad, eh,' she said. 'I thought you are a pervert, but now I see ...' She looked down at where my legs ended.

Her face crinkled into a smile, her lips a little lop-sided, her eyes black, melting. Below her eyes ran a few more wrinkles than I had seen through my telescope. I made way for her, but still could find no words. I wheeled myself to the window, where the two telescopes stood.

'I'm sorry,' I managed after a long minute. I could sense her standing right beside me, her warmth seeping through my arms.

She walked about the room, taking in the sparseness. I'd never made any attempt to make my home anything other than functional.

'How long you been like this?' She walked to the front door, latching it shut. I hated how direct she was, but liked it at the same time. She stepped toward me, not flinching at the sight of my legs.

'None of your business,' I turned away.

'You're a good one to talk about that!' she turned my wheelchair around to face her. Her nose flared in anger, but her eyes grew moist.

'This is why I don't meet people. I'm not one of your soap operas ...' I began, bile rising in my throat.

Look at your game, girl... Axl Rose whined from the speakers.

'But I am your soap opera, right? You know I watch serials on TV. You see me cry. You can spy on people when you want, but the minute ...'

'I'm sorry,' I said again, and this time I meant it. Having telescopes did not give me the right to do what I did. *Sad, sad, maaaad game*, Rose wailed, and I wanted to get up and shut him off.

'I meant we're all human. Different things work for different people,' she murmured against my ear. The window darkened, and I felt her lips on my face, caught a whiff of jasmine as her long, straight hair curtained about me.

She stroked my jaws, worked her way down to my throat, my chest, as she took off my shirt, biting my neck. 'Let's have some fun, okay?' she whispered.

I sat there, mute with shock. I had dreamt up similar scenarios a dozen times, got off on them, without any hope of them ever turning real. And now here she was.

She stood up, turned the wheelchair towards the black leather couch. I could have moved the wheelchair myself, but I let her do it. I lay on the couch and watched her instead. The next I knew my boxers had fallen to the floor. Her right hand flitted down between my legs. With her left hand, she touched whatever was left of my legs, first time in eight years someone had done that. She did not shrink from the pinkish, rounded stumps I had turned away from hundreds of times in the mirror.

I saw her undressed, slim waist fanning into wide hips. But instead, a frilly, butterfly-printed cotton top worn over shorts stared back at me. Maybe she should have dressed her age. My attention wandered as her fingers flitted between my legs and she declared, 'Well, you sure got what it takes. I think we could be friends.'

Half-sitting, half-lying down, I gripped the couch with both hands. She got lost in her own pleasure, not knowing I lay beneath her. She stopped only to pull out a condom from her brown-and-black Louis Vuitton bag. Her need frightened me. Like a dark cave on an unexplored island, it called to me but offered no promise of return.

When I did emerge, I didn't feel so bad. After she washed up and left, I drew up a mental list of things I knew about her.

Lili could be her real name or a fake; I did not know her surname. I knew her boyfriend (had to be the *ang moh*, because no one else visited her) was my neighbour. That is why he looked so familiar – I must have seen him on one of the rare trips I made outside, but not remembered. I shoved that thought aside and focused on her.

'Aren't you scared your boyfriend will find out about this?' I asked her after a few visits. By now, she had told me she worked at the Sentosa aquarium as a cleaning supervisor and that her American boyfriend worked at the same place as the dolphin trainer. Their work schedules matched, so she showed up at my place when he went out with the other *ang moh* boys.

'Isn't fear of being found out half the thrill? No one knows that better than you!'

I nodded, partly because my mouth had found better things to do than talk.

'I like you,' she said, 'you never say no to anything. And you're so ... different.' She struggled for another word, then gave up. 'You'll never give me a bag like that one,' she continued, pointing at her Louis Vuitton, 'but that's okay.' She dipped into her bag to pick up a condom and fit it in place. Her hands gripped my stumps as she levered herself on top of me.

I did want to speak up right then, but kept quiet. She had rescued me from my eight-year celibacy.

'Say my name,' she said, her thighs rising and falling, straddling me, 'we'll have fun today. I have goodies in my bag, you'll see.'

I looked into her eyes, but did not obey her.

'Lili,' – she bent over me – 'call me Lili,' and when I still did not speak, she pushed at my shoulders with both hands. 'I need to hear my name.'

This annoyed me. Not only did I feel out of practice and nervous about coming too soon, I had never vocalized during sex before, or been ordered about by a woman. Izzy Stradlin and Axl seemed to agree, growling and menacing my speakers, as they launched into *Back off bitch*. But Lili wasn't done. She pulled my hands from her hips and drew them to her neck. 'Press hard.'

'No!' It came out guttural, hoarse.

'Yes.' Her voice cold, steady. 'That is the only way I come.'

'OK.'

'You must say, "OK, Lili". I tell you before. Call my name!'

I could still hear her over Stradlin's thundering guitar, so she must've been shouting. Her face remained calm though.

I closed my mouth. My mind wanted one thing, my body another. I had never been submissive before. But the moist cave of her desire sucked at me exactly as if she had a tongue down there, a tongue that pressed and mated with me at all the right spots, making me wish to live in that darkness, never come back to light.

But Lili lifted her body off mine, letting in the freezing air from the air-conditioning, and I began to lose my erection. In that blast of cold air, I suffered all the hours of loneliness of the past few years, the longing to talk to someone, hold a woman in my arms, bury myself in her.

Face of an angel with the love of a witch ... blasted Rose from the speakers. At that moment, I hated Lili.

'OK, Lili, whatever you want.' I closed my eyes as she swirled her tongue on me before impaling herself again. She held my hands and put them about her neck. I stroked her throat with my thumb, feeling one horizontal line cutting across it, and below it, another. As I pressed a little, a pulse raced under the skin, just below her jaw.

'Press hard!'

I held her but added no pressure. She reached out to her handbag and pulled out a black plastic packet. It crackled as she opened and put it over her head, making her look like an abused prison-camp inmate.

'Now!'

Knowing I might do some real damage, I gripped her throat a little harder than before, but not much. I dipped my fingers over the plastic and ran my thumb in small circles.

'Not like that – I need some strength.' Lili moved faster.

'And I'll tell you when it is enough.'

'How?' By this time, I wanted to slap her off me and be done with it.

'I'll dig my nails in your arms like this,' she growled in my ear. She pressed the half moons of her nails so hard into my arm, I winced. 'I may pass out for a bit, but that's normal, okay?' Her voice jarred, but I ignored it, and tried to focus on the guitar strings in the background instead.

'OK.'

'Go!'

Her voice had the crack of a bullet at the start line of a race. She picked up more pace. I closed my eyes, not liking the way her nose peaked under the black plastic hovering over me.

But with eyes closed, my brain called up for me that same strangled-calf look she had with her boyfriend. She must have controlled him then, just as she was controlling me now, while looking the terrified victim.

She gripped my hands, urging me on. I could feel the tension building up, and knew I would explode soon – if pain was what she wanted, that's what she would get. I gave it all I had.

Her hips slackened their pace, shuddered and tightened about my loins with her release. In the throes of my orgasm, I held on, gripping and clutching as I came.

When I opened my eyes, Lili had gone limp. I laid her gently down on me, taking the plastic off her head, smoothing back her hair.

As my heart slowed its hammering, I felt a peculiar stillness. It was not the post-coital calm I was growing used to in the last few weeks, nor the strains of *November Rain* that had now begun to play.

Lili's body on top of me felt heavy, and I pushed her a little to the side. Her head lolled on to her bag, making it roll over and spill her things. Something slipped to the floor and dropped with a thunk; a metal collar. Her body no longer joined mine. She had passed out. Her legs fell to the floor at awkward angles like that of an accident victim. I propped myself up on my arms, and stretched out to gather her to myself.

'Lili?' I tapped her cheek with my fingers as I lifted her.

But she did not answer. When I put my hands around her neck to lift her head, I felt no pulse under her jaw. I put my ears to her chest, heard no beat. Panicked, I shook her, but her body moved in all directions at once.

I let myself fall from the couch, dragged myself to the wheelchair, jammed its wheels, and clambered up. I went to the kitchen, filled a glass of water and splashed it on Lili's face. Her skin looked ashen, as if someone had slipped a sheet of carbon paper beneath it.

I stared at her for a while, not sure what to do. I wheeled myself to the wireless phone, picked it up, but almost immediately put it back on the cradle. The jasmine of her hair filled my head, making it impossible to think, and then under the perfume, I imagined I smelled something gone bad.

No one would have seen her. The corridor was empty when I let her in, and no camera covered my door. The footage at the lobby camera would show her enter the building. But I remembered that she always came unannounced, without any word on the intercom from the guards. So she must have had an access card ... I rifled through the bag and found it. I breathed easier then, because she could have just as easily been visiting her boyfriend next door.

Before I could think further, I went to the living room, wiped Lili down with tissues. I switched off the lights and wheeled myself to the balcony, her body on my lap. No one in my condominium could see me, and unless the HDB apartment opposite harboured a telescope enthusiast, I could get away with it. I heaved Lili's body upwards and shoved it over the balcony parapet. I wheeled myself in and pulled the glass shutters closed.

* * *

It has now been six months since the last time Lili left this building. The neighbourhood was in an uproar for a few weeks after her death, and the boyfriend still remains the main suspect. The police made their rounds, asked me a few normal questions, but didn't look though my apartment. If they had, my training would have saved me. I put my telescopes in storage. I knew not to leave any evidence lying around. Or perhaps not. I've kept that LV handbag.

I know I should get rid of it, flush its ashes just like I did with everything else from that night – the condom, the black packet, the tissues. But I haven't got down to it yet. Instead, I take it out from time to time, running my hands on the leather, laying out the things it contains: a tube of Endless Red L'Oreal lipstick, tissues, a packet of condoms, a steel-weave collar with a padlock, a coiled whip. After a while, I put the things back one by one. That bag knows exactly what I've done, and will tell anyone who bothers to ask.

But I feel it has stayed behind with another purpose: so I

can use its contents. There has to be a reason why the *ang moh* had no good alibi, why no one came looking for me; perhaps destiny has other plans. I'll have to be more careful next time. The challenge would be to find a lure, because matter-of-fact girls like Lili are rare. I'm sure I can think of something.

The strings of *November Rain* no longer soothe me. For now, it's time I returned to my binoculars and telescope. They've been gathering dust far too long.

D. Biswas loves reading books, observing people, and drinking tea. She tinkers around with people in stories, trying to figure out what makes them tick, because she can't do that in real life. She asks 'what if?' every time something out of the ordinary catches her eye. She has published a bunch of stories, and is now tinkering with the people in her first novel. Find out more about her at Amloki.com.

Singapore

ROAD KILL

RICHARD LORD

Kannan Katt had been working as a Singapore police force inspector for just under three months and he still didn't feel that he fit in. Soon after his assignment to the Cantonment headquarters, he had determined that the police force was a kind of club, bound by its own set of rules. But he had not yet mastered all the rules. In fact, he was still deeply in the dark about what many of those rules were.

Still feeling awkward, he strolled into the fifth-floor canteen with Sergeant Faizal, his colleague from Criminal Investigation Division, for a late-morning coffee.

From across the room, the two were invited to join a few uniformed officers at their table. The officer who had signalled the invitation was Hamilton Kwan, a cheerful fellow in his late forties who was friendly towards Kannan.

Faizal was still at the counter, waiting for a heated-up

muffin to go with his coffee as Kannan sat down with his. He was greeted with one of Kwan's impromptu lectures.

'Hey, Kannan, you know we're getting almost as exciting over in the Traffic Division as you guys up in CID. We just got another fatality. Some fool slammed a pedestrian in the crosswalk because he wasn't paying attention. Second one like that in two weeks, too. Both victims dead on the scene: bang, boop, splat, all over.'

'So what happened?' asked the Malay officer to Kwan's right whom Kannan did not know.

'The driver said he was "distracted for just a moment". Distracted; you know what he was doing? He had one of those things that runs videos next to the steering wheel and he was watching one of those instead of the road. A pedestrian starts crossing and interrupts the film by getting hit.'

'Getting splattered, more like,' added the officer next to Kwan.

'Oh, shit.'

Kannan tried to judge what his exact response should be and then register this on his face. He decided on a wince. 'And this is the second one like that?'

Kwan nodded. 'A week ago last Tuesday, a guy is listening to music while he's backing up. He's changing the channel, keeps backing up, not looking, hits a pedestrian walking behind him, drags him along ten metres, doesn't even know the guy's there until he feels "something dragging" under the car.'

Kannan now delivered his full-winged wince. 'Not a pleasant way to go.'

Kwan gave a look that was half grimace, half smile. 'Even

you wouldn't want to hear the details.'

And then, as if they were the two players in a rehearsed routine, Kwan's colleague on his right provided those details.

'His neck was snapped right across, spine twisted, hip broken, skull smashed, bit of brain left on the street.' Staff Sergeant Lee finished the litany with a sour expression and sad nod of the head, suggesting that those were the highlights.

Kwan shook his head in tandem. 'The worst thing, you know, is how easy these guys get off. You kill someone with a car, it's an accident, all we can charge them with is negligent driving. You get maybe a $5,000 fine and they suspend your driving privileges for two years, max.'

'You're kidding," said Kannan.

'No. The most you can get … three years suspension and a $10,000 fine, but you have to be really negligent to even get that.' He flicked an irritated finger against his coffee cup. 'I think we would get better drivers if we made the penalties stronger. Give them about a dozen strokes of the cane, they kill somebody. The cane, the fine and no driving for at least five years. Then I think these guys would start paying more attention when they're at the wheel.'

'At least that,' the Malay officer to Kwan's left said in agreement.

Sergeant Faizal, having joined the group, stared off as if in a fantasy. 'Five thousand dollars fine, two year suspension. You know, if I ever really want to kill somebody, I think I'll just run them over with my car. Call it an accident, say I was looking the wrong way.'

The older Malay officer laughed. 'Yeah; you just say you were staring at some really good-looking girl, everyone will believe it. They all know you too well.'

All the cops laughed at this. But Kannan Katt's laugh came late and was offered mostly as follow-up to the other laughs. He hadn't really been listening to that exchange. His own thoughts had already jumped to what they were joking about. And he wasn't thinking of a joke.

As soon as he got back to his office, Kannan plunked himself into his chair, grabbed a small blue notebook and started jotting down notes. Not two minutes later, he was out of his seat, pacing back and forth, like a panther sensing some prey in the distance and already calculating how best to attack. After several rounds back and forth, he grabbed his phone and dialled the exchange of Kwan from the Traffic Division. He got his first break on the case right there: Kwan was in his office and answered after four rings.

'Kwan here.'

'Hamilton, this is Katt, Kannan Katt.'

'Oh, Kannan. What can I do for you, sir?'

'Funny you should ask. I was just wondering if you could ... do me a favour.'

'Let's hear it.'

'Do you happen to have the statements from those two drivers involved in the fatal accidents. The ones you were talking about in the canteen?'

'Sure; we have full statements. Why?'

'I was hoping I could maybe ... take a look at them? They might be able to help me with a case we're trying to patch together over here.'

'OK, that shouldn't be any problem. Anything else you'd

like to look at? We can give you some background on the two guys, descriptions of the accidents, whatever.'

'That would be great. I would really appreciate that. We would ... all appreciate that. It could be very helpful.'

'OK, give me about half an hour, I'll try to put everything together that I can let you look at.'

Half an hour later, almost to the minute, Inspector Katt was at Kwan's office to pick up a slender file filled with reports on the two separate fatal accidents. Kwan had gone out, but an assistant dutifully handed Katt the file, along with a brisk smile and no questions asked.

That afternoon, Kannan was at his computer, staring intensely at the screen, hoping to find something he could add to his findings. He was so absorbed, and so frustrated, that he hadn't noticed one of the Division's senior officers, Inspector Lim, who had shuffled in and planted himself right behind Katt. After a few seconds, Katt became aware of this stealthy presence, and turned around with an embarrassed look on his face. Inspector Lim returned that look with a strained smile steeped in vitriol.

'This is .. uhh, Facebook. It's what they call a social networking website.'

'Yeah, I know what the Facebook is,' Lim replied. 'My two kids waste most of their time with that thing.' He tapped the sheath of papers he was carrying against his leg as he cleared his throat. "Maybe nobody's spoken to you about this before, Inspector, but we do not like our officers surfing the Internet and doing other personal things during work hours.'

'No, I know that, Inspector Lim. Thank you for the reminder, but this is nothing personal. I was doing research for a crime investigation.'

'Oh? What case is this then?'

'Well, it's not really a case yet. As such. But I think it could be. And an important case really. But I'm still trying to put things together, to work out a possible double homicide here.'

Lim shook his head in incredulity. 'Inspector Katt, we don't try to spin out murder cases in this division. We wait for real murders to happen, and then we go out and solve them and arrest the perpetrators.

'Now I realise working in a low-crime jurisdiction like ours might be a little bit boring for someone like you who went to university and likes to read lots of literature. But here we like to concentrate on what we have before us, not go out and make some case that doesn't even exist yet.'

'I understand, Inspector Lim. And thank you for that reminder as well.'

'No problem. Oh, here are the latest figures and assessments from the Division administrator. You can study these if you're very bored.'

'Thank you, Inspector. I'll start studying right away.'

'Yes, that's good. Right after you turn off that Facebook thing.'

Katt clutched the mouse tensely and clicked to close the Facebook page. He hadn't been able to find what he was looking for, but he knew he could search again later, maybe when he got home.

The next morning, Inspector Katt still hadn't found what he was searching for in Facebook, but he had found an interesting snippet in the report on one of the accidents. He circled that with a red pen and switched his energy flow to following this lead.

* * *

Early the next week, Katt decided to go to the most senior officer in his group with what his investigation had turned up. He knocked on Deputy Superintendent Weston Tan's door, having called earlier to ask if he could see him briefly.

'Kannan, come in, come in. How are you this morning?'

'I'm fine, sir. And how are you?'

After hopping through the pleasantries, they got down to business. They were both men who liked getting down to business quickly.

Kannan told that the Deputy Superintendent he'd been looking at the two fatal traffic accidents in the past few weeks and he noticed something suspicious. One of the drivers, he informed his superior, had profited significantly from the death of one of the pedestrians involved.

'What?? A man profits big from the death of somebody he's killed with his vehicle, and Traffic doesn't see anything strange in that?'

'The thing is, sir, that driver didn't kill the man whose death benefited him.'

'But I thought you just said …'

'No, that fortunate fellow was the driver in the second fatality. The man whose death greatly benefited him was the victim in the first incident.'

'Oh. So what is the case here?'

'I don't think either death was really an accident.'

'Oh?'

'I'm pursuing a hunch that the two drivers were somehow involved in a pact. That the first one killed the other man's target intentionally and the second driver then killed the first driver's target to fulfil his part of the deal.'

'Sounds complicated, Kannan. Sounds very complicated.'

'Which is why I think it might be true. The two perpetrators would assume that it was so complicated, they could get away with two murders. But we can still foil them if we can work out the deal they came up with and how the deaths are related.'

Deputy Superintendent Tan rested the lower part of his face in a folded fist and slipped into rumination for a short time. When he pulled his hand away from his face, he seemed to have reached a decision.

'So you want approval from me to pursue this further?'

Katt took a calming breath before answering. 'That's right, sir.'

'Alright. I give you my approval. Also any office support you might need. But on one condition: you need to have a senior officer working with you on this investigation.'

'Yes, I already anticipated that, sir.'

'Fine. I assign you to work with Inspector Lim on this.'

'Inspector Lim?'

'Yes. Is there a problem there?'

'Uhh … no, not really a problem. It's just that … I'm not sure that Inspector Lim would be all that sympathetic to this case. Or to …'

'To you?' Tan nodded sympathetically. 'I understand your hesitation, Inspector Katt. I know that Inspector Lim often takes a while to warm up to new people in the Division. And he is suspicious of some people who have taken … an easier path to success.'

'Easier, sir?'

'Look: you got out of the academy with a glowing record and in about two days, you reached a level that it took Lim twelve years to work his way up to. I know he's suspicious that someone can learn enough in police courses as they can being out there doing the hard work. But he is one of our best men. And he's a lot smarter than he likes to let on.

'Even better, he's got long years of good, practical experience investigating crime he can call on. If this investigation is going to go anywhere, Lim is the best person to help you with it. Inspector, I want you to work with him on this, because I want you to be successful with it. That's my decision. Any questions?

'No, sir, no questions.'

'Well then, thank you for your work so far on this matter and good luck with your investigations.'

'Thank you, sir.'

Inspector Katt sat in his office for over an hour mulling his decision. Was there any way he could get around bringing Lim into this investigation, maybe with another officer or two and using Lim as a figurehead? When he finally realized that he had no other option if he wanted to pursue this case, he swallowed hard and trudged down the hall to see Lim. He brought all his research with him in a large manila envelope.

He knocked on the door and waited until Lim barked permission to enter. Usually, CID officers just knocked twice and looked in on fellow officers, but Katt was sure that Lim would be looking for any excuse to turn him and his project away.

He began his narrative by saying that he had the lead on an extremely interesting case, and that Deputy Superintendent Tan agreed with him that it was interesting. In fact, he dropped the deputy superintendent's name four times in his short introduction. Inspector Lim still had a sour look on his face, as if ingrained scepticism tasted like sliced lemons. But he did ask Katt to go on. Katt felt he just had to build up his momentum and deliver a strong argument.

'OK, I think I have a double homicide here.'

'When? Superintendent Tan didn't say nothing about this to me.'

'That's what we have to prove, that it was homicide. In fact, that's what I was trying to put together that one day last week. Remember, when you walked in on me, and I was on Facebook?'

'Yes, I remember that. I remember very well.'

'OK, here's what I've been working on. Did you ever watch the film *Strangers On A Train*?'

Lim scrunched his features. '*Strangers On a ...*? No, I don't think so.'

'It's a film by Alfred Hitchcock. A real classic.'

'Oh. No, then I haven't watched it. I don't like all those classic things.'

'This one you would like, I'm pretty sure. OK, here's the story: These two guys meet on a train. They're perfect strangers, never met before.'

'OK.'

'The one guy, he's a big tennis star. Like Roger Federer.

'I prefer Rafael Nadal.'

'OK, Nadal then. Anyway, he's this famous tennis star. He's got everything going for him. He's really handsome, charming, everything. He's in love with this lovely girl, she's the daughter of an American senator, and they want to get married.' Lim nodded. 'But they can't, because the tennis star is already married. And his wife is a real bitch who won't give him a divorce.'

'I know the type.'

'The other stranger, he's the son of a really wealthy man. But the son, he's an absolute slacker, obnoxious, wants everything handed to him.'

Lim nodded. 'I know that type, too.'

'Anyway, he hates his father and his father hates him, the father's just about to disinherit him, cut him off without a penny.'

'Cheers to the father.'

'Now, the rich guy, he suggests to the tennis star that they make a secret pact: the rich punk kills the star's wife, but then the tennis star has to kill the rich guy's father for him.'

'Why?'

'That's just it. There doesn't seem to be a why. The two intended victims are both complete strangers to the other person. The tennis star seems to have no motive to kill the spoiled guy's rich father, and the rich guy has no motive to kill the tennis player's wife. So he thinks it's a perfect crime; a perfect double crime, in fact. No one will suspect the two murderers because neither one has any motive to kill the person they kill. They swap motives, and then they swap murders.'

'OK, and how is this relevant to us?'

And it was then that Lim sat back and crossed his arms

tightly over his chest. Katt felt the wind drawn out of his momentum. Crossed arms held high on the chest: Body Language 101 tells you this person has just shut the doors on what you want to tell him. Lim had already decided to be uncooperative, Kannan told himself. He knew this would not be an easy sell, but he didn't think that his attempt would be shut down this quickly. Still, he had to give it a shot as he was fairly sure it was important.

'Those two people killed in the so-called negligent driving incidents?'

'Yeah …?'

'I think both of them were non-accidents. I'm saying that both of them were intentional, well-planned murders. The only thing is, the two killers swapped the people they wanted to kill and swapped motives. The first driver killed the second driver's victim, and the second driver killed the first one's victim.'

'And what proof you have on this?'

The junior inspector swallowed deeply. 'Right now, it's just a theory swimming around, looking for proof.'

Lim's eyebrows swept up again into their full sceptical height. But Katt was not ready to give up yet.

'And until yesterday, it was just an interesting theory. Today, it's a strong theory.'

'I see. Why?'

Katt picked up the piece of A2 paper on the side of his desk, unfolded it, and spread it out on the desk. He'd sketched out some diagram on that paper and now started to explain it to his colleague.

'The second driver knew the first victim. More than that, they were both involved in this really convoluted … really mixed-up inheritance case.' Kannan paused and sucked in air. Was it even worth going on now? Lim's response took him by surprise.

'OK, I'm still interested.' And as if to prove that, Lim had unfolded his arms, put his hands on the desk and leaned forward to get a better look at the diagram.

'Driver number two was a nephew by marriage of this rich guy who died in January. Victim number one was his blood nephew.' Lim nodded. 'Driver number two seemed to have inherited a handsome chunk from our wealthy guy. But the blood nephew took out a suit stopping him from getting what he was supposed to get. He was contesting that part of the will. Even more relevant is that it looked like he might have a good case. At least good enough to delay settlement for a year, maybe two years.'

'How much was involved?'

'Our lucky driver should now get about $600,000.' Lim pursed his lips in respect of the amount. 'And also two condos. On the east coast.'

'OK. This is starting to sound promising. And what was driver number one's motive for wanting the other victim dead?'

'That's the glitch,' said Kannan. 'I just haven't figured that one out yet.' The young inspector felt like an angler who had just lost his catch. But to his surprise, Lim did not react negatively to this admission.

Lim stared down briefly and intensely at Katt's diagram, as if he might be able to read something there that Katt himself had missed. After ten very long seconds, Lim looked back up. 'No motive?'

'None ... that I've been able to find yet.'

Lim stared back down at the diagram, then shook his head. 'Inspector Katt, this could all be just a great coincidence, you know.'

'It could be. Yes, it is maybe possible it's all coincidence.' He paused for effect. 'Do you think it is a coincidence? Do you *really* think this is a coincidence?'

Lim squinted hard, as if this allowed him to see something otherwise closed off to him.

'You really need to find that second motive. Without that, we can't move very far on this thing.'

Kannan looked at him intently. 'We? As in you and me?'

The look on Lim's face suggested he was already thinking ahead, to the next steps they would need to take. 'Let's see if we can find that motive for driver number one.'

Kannan flashed a big smile, but Lim merely stared back down at the diagram. Then, a few moments later, he looked up, nodded, and the two officers shook hands. Lim now had an inquisitive look.

'And how'd you come up with this information about the inheritance and the legal fight over it?'

'I ... that's what I've been doing research on for the last ... few days.'

'Just on a wild hunch?'

'Yah, it was kind of ... just on a hunch.'

Lim nodded. 'Good work.' He then turned and reached for some papers on his desk. He started going through the papers without turning back to his visitor. Katt knew it was time for him to leave with no more ado.

Within the next half-hour, Drivers Number One and Two

had been given their proper names: Driver One was Ong Swee Chun and Driver Number Two was Daniel Tay. Lim learned the victims' full names as well. Katt also handed over photocopies with a quick background on victims and suspects. Though reluctant to admit it, Lim was hooked.

* * *

For the next three days, Inspectors Katt and Lim worked hard trying to link Ong to the death of the second victim, one Andrew Lee.

'Why would Ong want to see this guy dead?' Inspector Lim kept asking, as if repeated cadences of this mantra would sluice out an answer. It didn't, and the repetition quickly started to irritate Inspector Katt, though he kept his irritation hidden; but only just.

Meanwhile, Katt did much of the legwork and came up with a raft of information on both Ong Swee Chun and the victim, but none of it suggested any link between Ong and the killing.

'Let's see, why do people kill other people? I mean, you know, a planned killing, nothing spontaneous.' Lim scrunched his brow. 'Greed, revenge, jealousy. Let's start with greed. That always seems to be a strong motivation here in Singapore.'

Katt pursed his lips before speaking. 'Nothing that we can determine would drive Ong to want the victim dead. We checked all his financials. No connection whatsoever to Lee. And he seems to have no financial problems. In fact, the one thing that stuck out recently was a big loan he got and a REITS deal.'

'Who was that with? Maybe it was a friend of this Daniel Tay. Or an enemy.'

Katt shook his head slowly. 'A bank. United Helvetica Bank, to be specific.' Lim scrunched his brows. 'It's the local branch of a Swiss bank. They're heavy in investments, but they also do some personal loans. I checked it all out. Ong secured a big loan from them last month, but he seemed to have no problem getting the loan. And he has no co-signer on it.'

'So no alarm bells ringing?'

'I'm afraid not.'

'OK. Hey, you think it might be a love triangle there? Andrew Lee was sleeping with Ong's wife maybe?'

Katt shook his head. 'Ong divorced his wife in 1998. And he doesn't seem to have had any serious relationships since then.'

'Maybe he divorced her because of this guy Lee. So then he waits seven years and takes his revenge. What's that they say about revenge? It tastes best, you eat it cold.'

Kannan again shook his head. 'She was the one who filed for divorce. And the reason given was irreconcilable differences. No mention of adultery anywhere in the court case. No mention on either side.'

Inspector Lim nodded. 'So, no love triangle. Too bad. I always like them. Lots of hanky panky in those triangles. Always makes a case more fun to work out.'

'I'm sure it does,' said Katt morosely. Suddenly he sat up stiffly. 'Wait a minute: a triangle. That could be it! Maybe Ong didn't want to see the victim dead, but someone else did. A someone else connected to Ong.'

'What?'

'We've been trying to find a nice, tidy, easy solution for a complicated case. A simple tit-for-tat: Ong's target for Tay's. But maybe it was more than that. Ong had a deal with someone else to kill Andrew Lee. Now we have to find out who that deal was with.'

'OK, I like that. So we start by ...' Lim looked at Katt as would a teacher looking to see if the star pupil had done his advanced homework, learned some key principle and could now solve the problem himself. Katt nodded.

'We talk to the widow. See if she has any idea who would want her husband dead.'

Lim nodded, a big smile on his face. He was proud of the student.

* * *

The next day, shortly before ten, Lim and Katt appeared at the front door of the apartment in Bukit Timah where Sondra Seow, Andrew Lee's widow, lived. Ms Seow was clearly surprised by the visit, and even more so when Inspector Lim stepped forward and flashed his police ID. He tried to give her a friendly smile mixed with appropriate sympathy. As Lim was not good at casting such mixed facial expressions, Sondra Seow's hesitant response was to be expected.

'Ms Seow, my name is Inspector Lim. This is my colleague, Inspector Katt.' Katt nodded. 'We'd like to ask you a few questions if it's not too much of a problem.'

'Well, actually, I was just getting ready to go out and ...'

'Just a few questions, I promise. It won't take more than five or ten minutes of your time.'

Sondra took a deep breath, nodded and invited the two policemen in. Two minutes later, the three were sitting across from each other in the tastefully decorated living room which the late Andrew Lee used to share with his wife. The two officers had passed up the offers of a drink, but Sondra Seow had gone into the kitchen to fetch a sports drink for herself. Lim waited until she returned, then started asking his carefully prepared questions. But even before he started, the widow put up a shield.

'I've already spoken to the police, you know. Twice.'

'Yes, yes, we know. That was our colleagues, Constable Kwek and Sergeant Haziz. But we just wanted to …'

'Ask questions of a slightly different nature,' Katt chimed in helpfully.

'Yes, that's it. A slightly different nature of question.'

'Well, alright, I guess. You're already here, you might as well ask.'

Lim nodded in gratitude, then struck a note of dramatic pause before commencing. 'Ms Seow, did your husband have any enemies that you know of?'

'Enemies? No, he didn't have any enemies.'

'That you know of.'

'Correct. No enemies that I know of.' She paused and moistened her bow-shaped lips. 'My late husband was a man who was fairly easy to get along with. Most people found him quite pleasant, and they liked him. And … nobody really disliked him. Not in a way to kill him.'

'Did he owe anybody money? A substantial amount?' At this, Ms Seow scrunched her face tartly, implying that she either didn't understand the question or couldn't believe that

Lim was sitting there asking it. 'Or did somebody else owe him money?'

'No. Again, not that I know of. And I think I would know. If a man has big money problems, he won't be able to hide it. Not from his wife. There are all those signs. I never saw any of that with my husband.'

Lim again nodded sympathetically. 'I understand.'

Katt also nodded sympathetically. But then he homed in with the payload question. 'Ms Seow, it is at all possible that your husband was … having a relationship with another woman? A sexual relationship?'

At this, anger flared in Seow's face and she sat up stiffly. She then glared at both officers – Katt first, then Lim.

'Have you no sense of decency? Don't you remember that I just lost my husband? Lost him in a terrible, senseless accident. And you have the nerve to ask me questions like that.' She then grabbed the bag sitting on the floor next to her and stood up angrily. 'I'm sorry, officers, but I'm just not able to deal with these matters right now.'

Lim reacted first: he stood, dipped his head in apology and offered her a wince of remorse. 'Yes, of course, Ms Seow. You're right; this is not a good time to be asking these kinds of questions. Also, we caught you at a strange time. I'm very sorry for this intrusion. Maybe some other time we can pick up with our … inquiries.'

This seemed to lower her hackles a bit. 'Yes, alright; perhaps at some other time. And now, gentlemen, if you'll excuse me, I have to get along with some other matters.'

'Yes, of course,' Inspector Lim assured her. 'We understand entirely, Ms Seow.' He again nodded in remorse, and a few seconds later, the two officers stood and headed to the front door without waiting for the lady to accompany them.

As they waited for the lift, Lim snapped his fingers in exasperation and made an irritating noise with his lips. 'Well, that didn't go as well as we hoped, isn't it.' He shook his head and stepped into the lift with just a frustrated glance at his partner. Katt joined him and they both stood staring at the door as the lift descended.

After a few moments, Lim mentioned that he had conducted a good many bad interrogations in his career.

'Even worse than that one, I imagine.'

Lim looked at him with a sly smile. 'Oh, I wouldn't say that one was really bad. Actually, It went kind of well, I'd say.'

Katt, who had been looking straight ahead, wrapped in thought, turned back to the senior inspector. They'd just reached the ground floor. As the doors opened, he fixed Lim with a quizzical look.

The smile did not leave Lim's face. 'So, Inspector, what do you say we might have learned from that session?'

Katt stared at Lim, then turned away for a few seconds. Suddenly, a look of recognition appeared.

'You think we just found our third part of the triangle?' A smile now started to stretch across Katt's face.

Lim nodded. 'Yes, I think so; the grieving widow herself. I really think she's our link to the second murder.'

Katt's smile deepened. He, too, nodded. 'Yeah … right. The way she was reacting there. Everything. That wasn't really someone outraged at our insensitive questions.'

Kannan then stabbed the air with his index finger. 'It was the reaction of a guilty party.'

'Who realises someone has caught up with their deed. And that makes them very irritable,' Lim added.

Kannan again nodded. 'And it just struck me: she said no one hated him enough to kill him. We never mentioned anything about him being murdered until then.'

Another, deeper nod followed. 'She's the one who wanted her husband dead. And she probably had many good reasons for it.' This time, Lim tapped his young colleague on the shoulder to show his approval. 'OK, let us count the ways.'

'Right. And then let's find out how this all ties in with Ong.'

* * *

The first task proved the easier ... by far. Kannan spent most of the next two days investigating. Then, armed with the juicy fruits of his investigations, he strolled briskly into Lim's office.

Lim looked up from some papers, a crisp smile on his face. 'You look like someone with good news.'

'I think you can call it that. Our poor widow? She's not so poor. The late Andrew Lee had no siblings and his wife was his only close surviving family member.'

'Sounds interesting.'

'So she gets the apartment they were living in. Which, as we know, is in one of those new, very nice HDB areas.'

'Right.'

'The thing is, they upgraded to that place. They kept the other place, which they rent out. So that property belongs to her as well.'

'Well, that should all soften the blow of losing her husband.'

'It gets even more softening. His car is now hers, and the money he had in his bank account, around seventy thousand.'

'Oh, yes.'

'And ... here's the big part. Mr Lee was carrying a $200,000 life insurance policy. But with triple indemnity, if he met his end through an accident like the one that he had. In other words, three times the payout on that insurance policy.'

Inspector Lim threw his hands up triumphantly. 'Oh yes! Motive, motive, motive.'

'With a capital M and double exclamation points.'

Lim clapped his hands together. 'OK, now we just have to find what links her to Ong.'

'Actually, I was trying to look for links. Or at least some hints while I was doing this other research.'

'Investigation is the term we prefer over here, Inspector.'

'Yes, of course. I meant investigation. Now we can just concentrate on finding that link. It's got to be there.'

'I'm sure it is,' said Lim with an avuncular tone. Kannan smiled and nodded at this.

'You know,' Kannan said as he stood up and slid the photocopy with the figures towards Lim. 'Until now, I was never *really* sure. I mean, I really had this strong feeling in my gut that I was right. But somewhere at the back of my head was this nagging doubt. Maybe it was just a double coincidence that looked like it should be something more. But now I'm convinced that we've uncovered a clever double homicide involving three people. Now we just have to tie it all up.'

'And that we will do, sir. And we'll do it very quickly.' Lim tapped his fist on his desk. 'Let me just finish up what I was working on here and then I'll come join you in your office to work out how we proceed.'

Kannen nodded, turned and left. He felt very good.

But one week later, the pair had still not found a single piece of additional evidence that tied Sondra Seow to Ong Swee Chun. Everywhere they looked, the trail wound up cold and barren.

It wasn't that they didn't try. Most of their working day was spent trying to turn up anything, anything at all, that could link Ong to the widow Seow. They had even put in extra hours almost every day. And when Kannan went home at night, he would spend time doodling things on paper, trying to connect the two. Later, he would lie restless in bed, all the lights off, and work out possible scenarios in his head. But nothing seemed to come together. In the morning, he'd wake up exhausted, haunted by this case.

Early on, the two had sat in Lim's office, staring at a triangle posted on a cork board, trying to come up with some connection.

'Do you think they were having an affair? Do you think that's what she used to get him into the arrangement?'

Kannan turned. 'An affair? OK, look at her.' He pointed to her photo, pinned at the top of the triangle. 'Now look at Ong. And then the husband.' Lim nodded. 'Do you think a woman who looks like that is going to cheat on her husband, a fairly handsome guy, with someone who looks like Ong?'

'Well, stranger things have happened. You never know what's going to attract somebody.'

'Yeah, I know there's no accounting for taste. But this wouldn't be a matter of strange taste; this would have to be full-out perversion if she moved away from her husband to climb into bed with Ong.'

Inspector Lim gave his partner an acerbic grin, which told Katt that he had edged a little too close to offending his jowly, balding senior with that remark. He decided to avoid any such witty toss-offs in future.

*　*　*

Ten ragged days later, the two sat staring at the exact same diagram: the triangle with the three suspects at different corners and the two supposed murder victims underneath.

All they could come up with was a supposition: that Sondra Seow had somehow come into contact with Ong, a contact that they had managed to erase, and then offered him a nice chunk of her windfall to participate in the crossed murders. And then, of course, either Sondra or Ong had come into some now lost contact with Daniel Tay and persuaded him to participate. But if Sondra Seow had offered Ong Swee Chun a lot of money, the payment would have had to be delayed until long after the double murders, after all the trails had grown cold.

Lim shook his head and summarised their situation with a dry, morose tone. 'Maybe we won't get that key bit of evidence. We just won't be able to prove that connection or prove that part of the murders.'

'Which means that we can't prove one or the other.' Kannan slapped the side of the board hard, in anger. He then strode to the other side. 'If we can't prove their involvement, then we can never prove that Daniel Tay killed Andrew Lee intentionally. It was just an accident, and a great coincidence that the victim of the first accident was Tay's distant relative whose death he profited handsomely from.'

'Yes, that is our situation.' Lim then took a deep breath. 'Kannan, I really, really hate to say this, but … maybe it's time that we just stepped back from this case. Just left it alone for a while. Maybe something will turn up, help to tie the pieces together. But just staring at this damn pattern doesn't solve anything.'

Kannan looked like he was in real pain. 'Isn't there anything we can do? Maybe bring all three of them in for questioning, try to squeeze it out of them, or maybe fool them into revealing something?'

Lim shrugged. 'It's possible. They may even feel guilt and confess during the questioning. But it's more possible that they'll deny everything and then go back and make sure any evidence is well covered up or destroyed.'

He paused and weighed the options. 'We probably have a better chance if they think they got away with it and nobody suspects anything. They keep thinking that, they might get careless.'

He then put his fingers to his temples and started rubbing. 'This thing has been giving me headaches, and I hate having headaches.'

Kannan gave a laugh. 'It's been giving me headaches too, and I rarely got headaches before this. Now I get them every day.' He stopped and stared off into space. After a long, sour pause, he turned back to Lim.

'I'm sorry; I can't let this go. Not now. I need to find out how it all hangs together.'

'It's not there, Kannan. It's just not there. I mean, it

probably is there, but these people are too clever for us. They were able to come up with the perfect crime.'

'Remember what we learn during our training? There is no perfect crime.'

'Well, good enough to beat us this time.'

Kannan turned back and stared at the board. Neither of them spoke for over a minute. Finally, Kannan pointed at the triangle. 'No, we've got them. Almost. The problem is that there's something we don't see yet. Something that makes all the pieces fit together.' He stood staring in silence for another minute, and then was hit with an epiphany.

'You know what it is? What we didn't see?' He almost lunged at the board, getting there in one huge stride, then carefully poked at the top of the triangle. 'Sondra Seow doesn't *have* a direct connection to Ong. No, their connection is through her lover.' He traced a line with his finger, close to and parallel to the line they had already drawn on their diagram.

'Her lover is the one who has the connection to Ong, and he has enough influence over him to draw him into a complex murder scheme. It's not three degrees of separation – it's four degrees. Which is, of course, even a better scheme – by one degree.'

'Her lover?' Lim had a puzzled look on his face, as if he had been missing something going on for some time. 'And who's this lover?'

'That we don't know yet,' Kannan replied vigorously. 'But he's the link we're looking for. He's the one who can tie up this final part of the case.'

At this, Lim gave a moan, dropped his arms, folded, onto the table and dropped his head into the folded arms.

'OK, I know it sounds lame, but it all makes sense. Somehow.'

Without raising his head from the desk, Lim asked, 'How? How does it make any sense?'

'It's like with science. You know how they have these great breakthrough theories in science, these new discoveries.'

Lim looked up and gave a squirming shrug. 'Sorry; I was always terrible in Science.'

'No, I wasn't very good at it myself. But I do remember that some of the most important discoveries in science came when they had put together this brilliant theory, with just one key element missing. One part of this great puzzle. And what they would say is, we can't see it now, we don't really have proof for it, but it must be there. It must be there because that's the only thing that works. There has to a planet, a moon there, a virus back in the picture somewhere … because it needs to be there for everything else to make sense.

'Well, Sondra Seow's secret lover is that for us: he has to be there for everything else to make sense.'

At that point, Inspector Lim himself stood up and started pacing, but more slowly, in a cautious, heavy-footed manner. He didn't look at Katt, even as he started talking.

'Inspector Katt, that's a nice way of putting this together. And I'm sure that if you were making a scientific theory and you said, "This has to be there, because it's the only thing that works", you would be a hero. You will get some award, maybe a promotion to a really good teaching job.

'But our job is catching criminals. And then sending them to trial where they can be found guilty for their crimes and given their due punishment. And we can't do that with something that we can't put our fingers on, but it "has to be there". We will get ourselves a nasty scolding from the Attorney General's office, we tried to walk in with that argument.'

Katt shook his head. 'I'm not saying we will do that.'

This did not make Lim feel any better. 'And the sad thing about this case is if we don't have every single element, the whole thing falls apart. You told me this yourself, Inspector.'

'I know, I know. And I know we have to find this lover if we want to have a case. What I wish to argue here is that we now need to direct all our energies to finding this missing lover.' No sooner had Katt said that last sentence, than he built his lower lip. He was sounding like a lawyer, or at least a law student. He didn't want to lose any of Lim's cooperation by doing something like that.

But Lim didn't seem to mind. He thought for a moment, nodded, then asked, 'Do we have any leads?'

'Not at the moment, but ... I think we might want to call in some outside help on this.'

This suggestion clearly did rile the senior inspector. 'Outside help? Why do we need outside help?'

'We don't, of course ... but it may point us in the direction of the missing lover and leave us free to work out some other details of the plot.' He took a long, taut breath. 'I know somebody who's an expert in this field. He's an old friend of mine from ... way back. Let me see if he's free and if maybe he can give us some assistance in finding the lover.'

Lim didn't reply, other than by staring intently at the diagram on the board, then down at some papers on the table. It was over a minute later that he turned to Katt and said, 'OK; you probably should contact this friend and see what help he can give us.' Katt nodded gratefully.

A short time later, Katt was back in his own office and on the phone to an old friend from university. This old friend, Robert Lozario, was frequently touted as perhaps the best private detective in Singapore. The fact that much of that touting came from Lozario himself did not bother Katt too much. The two had once been quite close friends, and Kannan still had a lot of trust in the man.

After six rings, a voice message came on, saying that all the agents were busy on assignment at the moment, but if the caller would leave a message, someone from Sleuth and Truth Private Investigation would get back to them soon. The Inspector left his message, saying he wanted to speak to Mr Lozario specifically and that he would be available at the following number for the next few hours.

The return call came within thirty seconds. 'Kannan. Hey stranger, how's it going?'

'Robert, good to speak with you again.' After a quick volley of catch-up greetings and polite questions, Katt got down to business. He told his friend that the CID needed some key information about a suspect, and they were ready to give the assignment to an outside agency, such as Robert's. Of course, Kannan assured him, the Singapore Police Force would be ready to pay his standard fees and expenses for the investigation. Robert said he would be more than happy to take on the assignment.

The Inspector then gave Lozario the name and some other details of the investigation's target. While he was still going down the list, Lozario deftly cut in. 'Hang on a minute – this

Sondra Seow, she was married to that guy Anthony Lee or something.'

'Andrew Lee.'

'Yeah, that's right: *Andrew* Lee. He just got killed in a traffic accident, isn't it?'

'That's right. I guess it made a few ripples over in the news pool.'

'I believe so. Look, send me all those details you have and I'll get back to you soon.'

'OK; I'll send along everything I have in the next twenty minutes or so.'

'You've got my e-mail address, right? Well, just shoot me that information.'

Kannan was still typing in details about where Sondra Seow lived and worked, the name of her fitness club and various marginal matters when the phone rang again. It was barely five minutes after he had called Lozario. He picked it up.

'Inspector Katt.'

'Robert again. OK, I've got a lot of the information you're looking for.'

'What?'

'We work fast around here. Hey, how many times have I told you I'm the best private eye in Singapore. Maybe now you'll start believing me.'

'I'd better believe it now.'

The two made arrangements to meet at a quiet bar near the Cantonment Police Headquarters a few hours later. When Kannan entered the Dutton Road bar, Robert was already there, making his way through a bag of chilli peanuts. They quickly ordered two Heinekens and played a bit more catch-up before getting down to business. When the beers arrived, Kannan insisted on paying.

'This one's on me. The follow-up brew as well, if there is one. It's because of me you had to come out here.'

'No problem, buddy.'

'All the same. It's my treat. Besides, if I let you pay for anything here, I know it would appear on the expenses statement you send to our people. So I might as well pay now.'

'You know me well, Kannan.'

'Very well. And that's why I come to you for your expertise in sordid affairs.'

Lazario laughed. After a toast to good fellowship, they swung back into the business behind this meet-up.

'So you already knew something about this affair?'

Robert eased his glass away from his face and nodded. 'About a year ago, Mr Andrew Lee engaged our services. He had some strong suspicions his wife was involved in extramarital activities and he asked us to investigate. As it happens, that was one of our easier assignments.'

'Why?'

'Ms Seow and her male friend were not into heavy cover-ups. Within a fortnight, we had juicy photos and videos of PDAs in various locations.'

Kannan scrunched his brow. 'PDAs?'

'Public displays of affection. Though a lot of people in my field prefer to call them "pretty damaging assignations". We also put together a little log of several meetings at this fancy short-term hotel. She would arrive about ten minutes after him and leave ten minutes before.'

'And they weren't having a business conference, I take it.'

'I did have my doubts.'

'OK, so go on.'

'There's nowhere to go. I've reached the end of that tale. We presented our preliminary report to Andrew Lee, he thanked us, paid us and said he didn't want any more snooping.'

'Isn't that strange?'

'Not really. Often times, a spouse who's getting cheated on just likes to get a nice messy stack of evidence to throw in the cheater's face. Believe it or not, that alone is sometimes enough to bring the affair to an end. There's a lot of remorse, a flood of tears, a touching forgiveness and a vow to go forth and sin no more. Maybe that's what happened with Andrew and Sondra.'

'Hmmm.' Kannan looked and sounded disappointed.

'But if you like, and would care to commission a further investigation, I could give you a quick update on the status of that affair.'

'I would like that a lot. But we do need something very quickly.'

'By when?'

'The day before yesterday?'

'I think we can manage that. Seriously, let me see what we can put together in the next couple of days.'

'That would be wonderful.'

'I'll put my A-team on this one. And, of course, I'll be out there leading the team.'

'I expect nothing less.'

Robert nodded and took another draught of his beer. Then he spoke. 'So you're now thinking that Mr Lee's fatal accident was maybe not quite an accident.'

The Inspector hesitated for several beats before answering.

'Something like that.' He then gave Robert a look that said he didn't want to discuss that matter any further at the moment. They were still close enough that Robert read the look accurately and immediately. He merely nodded and returned to the task of downing his beer.

Two days later, Inspector Katt had received no communication from Robert or his agency. A call late in the afternoon of the second day drew no reply. Around 4 o'clock on the third day, Katt finally got the phone call he was waiting for.

'Kannan, it's your favourite snoop.'

'Robert. What have you got for us?'

'Something very, very interesting. When can we meet up?"

'As soon as possible.'

An hour later, they were again at the same bar and twinned Heinekens, freshly drawn, were on their way. Preliminaries were kept to a minimum this time, as Lozario could see his friend was anxious to get information.

'OK, I can't say what might have happened in the interim, but at the present time, the widow Seow is still in contact with that guy she was seeing last year.'

'You're sure?'

'Of course. As a matter of fact, they spent a few hours together just last night at a condo in the Novena area.' Lozario opened a notebook to a pre-marked page. 'From 7:42 to 10:56, to be exact.'

'That is exact. And who is this lover?'

'A guy called Axel Gersten.'

'Sounds German.'

'Close enough. He's a Swiss. He's one of the local directors of a major Swiss bank with operations here.'

Kannan gazed into the air as he spoke. 'United Helvetica Bank?'

'Exactly. How'd you know that?"

'It had to be. It's what had to be there.' He turned to Robert and stared him in the face. 'It's the final fit, the piece that fits and gives us the whole picture.' He slapped the table in triumph. 'You've got evidence of all this? Pictures and everything?'

'You could have a small gallery exhibition with all the photos and videos we've got on this.'

Kannan thrust both his hands into the air. 'Yes.' He put his arm around Robert's shoulder and gave him a big, robust squeeze. 'You *are* the best PI in Singapore. And you just helped us break this case.' He spread his arms apart as far as they would go. 'Break it wide open!'

Inspector Lim had already left the office, but Katt buzzed him on his mobile phone to tell him that he thought he had found the missing piece that proved their breakthrough theory. They discussed the who and what briefly, then agreed that they would meet at the office extra early the next day to start pulling everything together. That night, Kannan slept deeply and well, the first really decent sleep he'd had in over three weeks.

His sleep was so good that he overslept the next morning and was actually late, not early, getting to the office. But Lim forgave him when he heard the full breakdown of the breakthrough.

'So I think the key connection to Ong is through Axel Gersten. And that loan Ong got two months ago from

UHB? I'm pretty sure it's just a clever way of paying him for participating in the double murder. It's probably Sondra Seow or Gersten himself who will pay off the loan. The same thing with that REIT that he got from UHB.'

A big smile was splashed across Lim's face. This only stoked Kannan's good mood further. 'We got them! We really got them!'

Lim put his hand up at this pronouncement. 'Not yet, Inspector, not yet. What we got here is a strong theory supported by evidence; but it's still all circumstantial evidence. And we still have no idea about what connects Daniel Tay to Ong.'

His mood noticeably dampened, Katt turned and looked at the board once more. 'Oh shit, I almost forgot about that. We still need that, don't we?'

'Not to worry: if we were able to discover all this other stuff, I think it's just a matter of time before we discover that last connection.' He paused, the big smile returning to his face. 'In fact, Inspector, right now I have no doubt we will discover it.'

A few hours later, Kannan burst into Lim's office again. 'Guess what I just found out. The money that Daniel Tay inherited?'

Lim leaned back and smiled. 'It was tied up in a United Helvetica three-year account.'

This knocked Katt completely off stride. 'How long have you known this?'

'About an hour. I thought I should call you up and tell you right away, but then I decided to wait till you came bursting in here again. I thought it would be more dramatic.'

'I guess it was. And you know who was the bank's administrator on that account?'

'Let me guess. Our friend Axel Gersten.' Kannan gave him the thumbs-up signal. He then stepped over to the board with the double homicide diagram and carefully drew a thick line between Gersten and Daniel Tay.

'And that closes our triangle.'

'Yes, sir. But now we need to turn the evidence into proof.'

Kannan turned. 'Right. How do we do that?'

'Here's where you get to complete your education, dear Inspector. Now is when we bring them in for questioning. We bring in all four of them.'

'Don't we have the same risk of just forcing them to close tighter than a pillbox?'

'Not if we handle it right. And I'm going to show you how to handle it right.' This time, Lim's smile had a slight twist of the conman to it. 'The hardest part of a good investigation is hooking the right fish. You've got that part mastered. But another important skill is knowing how to reel that fish in. That's the next lesson.'

The pair spent the next two days working with others in the Force to draw up warrants and a tightly rehearsed strategy. On the third day, police arrived at the offices of Daniel Tay, Ong Swee Chun and Axel Gersten and the home of Sondra Seow. By 3 pm, all the suspects had been taken to the Cantonment complex and brought to the interrogation centre.

Ong Swee Chun was waiting in a small, side office sporting a grimace as Inspectors Lim and Katt approached. Lim pulled out his handphone at the door and punched a speed-dial number. Within seconds, he got an answer.

'OK, we're about to bring out our suspect. You start out with this Gersten guy.' Lim then looked into the room and asked Ong to join them across the hall in one of the interrogation rooms.

As the three of them were heading across the bullpen, another officer turned the corner with his suspect: Axel Gersten. The officer had a tight squeeze hold on Gersten's elbow; the coldly handsome Swiss did not look much happier than did the haggard Ong.

As they proceeded in opposite directions, the two groups 'happened to' pass within a foot of each other. Gersten saw Ong, then looked away quickly, pretending to neither know nor notice him. But Ong was obviously so startled when he saw Gersten that he stared at him the whole time they were passing each other.

'A friend of yours?' Inspector Lim asked. Ong's only response was to look at the two policemen with dismay before garbling a few words. He seemed unable to speak coherently all the way into the interrogation room.

A short time later, another police officer from the CID brusquely escorted Daniel Tay into an interrogation, but made the well-planned 'mistake' of bringing him into a room already occupied: by an Inspector Tal, who was grilling Alex Gersten. The fellow officer quickly apologized to Tal for interrupting the interrogation. But he also lingered a short time, extending his apology so as to allow Gersten and Tay to spear each other with caustic stares. When he pulled Mr Tay out and closed the door, Inspector Long found himself with a noticeably more cooperative suspect.

Inspector Katt stayed overtime again, banging out his reports on the case to date. Shortly before seven, his partner Lim knocked, then stepped in. He was toting three small grey boards. Katt looked at the boards, perplexed, and his perplexity only grew when Lim carefully arranged them on a side table: one on the bottom, the other two on the sides, like a small tent.

He looked up, smiled, then grabbed one of the side boards, which he pulled away swiftly. The tent, of course, collapsed.

'And that's the way it works,' Lim crowed. 'You pull out just one side of a triangle and the whole thing collapses.'

'What? You got them all to confess?' Kannan asked.

'All except Gersten. Ong cracked first, right after you left. "The whole thing was his idea, he pushed me into it" is what he said.'

'He was talking about Gersten, is it?' Kannan asked.

Lim nodded. 'But then he explained the whole swapped killings scheme to us. How they worked it out and everything. Not a bad job of planning, I got to admit. And when we told Tay what Ong had told us, he quickly cracked too, explained his part in the arrangement, and also put the blame on Gersten.

'We used all this in our interrogation of Sondra Seow, and the lovely widow broke down quickly. Really broke down, too. It wasn't too long before she was crying like a little child, saying how affectionate and understanding a husband Andrew Lee was and how she should never have allowed Gersten to talk her into this horrible deed.'

'And what does our banker friend say about all this?'

'Just what you'd expect from a very respectable businessman who has this interesting little sideline in having people killed.

He claims the other three are all highly delusional.'

'And that includes his girlfriend?' Katt asked with eyes spread wide.

'Oh, that was maybe the best part. He says he met that woman – that's what he called her, "that crazy woman" – at some corporate functions and she asked if he could advise her on some financial matters. He claims they met a few times to discuss investments and all like that, and then she started to make all these crazy suggestions. He also swore that their relationship was "strictly professional".'

Kannan tapped the thick envelope with the photos that Robert Lozario had provided. 'He has a very interesting profession then, I'd say.'

'You said it. Wish I could get into that field.'

'Think he might get away with it?'

'He's got about as much chance as I have to steal Angela Jolie from Brad Pitt.' Lim then lowered his eyelids and shook his head. 'We've got three signed confessions and three very scared witnesses all pointing their fingers in the same direction: at Mr Gersten. I don't think any judge here will buy the story he wasn't deeply involved in those killings.' Katt and Lim shared a volley of high-beam smiles at that.

But Katt then grew slightly sombre. 'Do you think they'll all hang?'

Lim shrugged. 'It depends. On a number of things. Look at it from one angle, they've all earned the right to hang. Look at it from another angle, they all can claim something that mitigates the sentence.' He shrugged. 'They might all hang, they might all get life sentences. One thing for sure: it will be a lot harsher than a $5,000 fine and loss of driving privileges for two years.' Katt gave a nervous laugh at that.

'Anyway, that's for the Deputy Prosecutor and the judge to decide. My job is just to catch bad people and turn them over to the courts, let them decide what happens to be justice in this case. Just catching bad people is work enough.' He paused a beat. 'As you know.'

There was an awkward silence in the room. Katt fingered the first pages of his report and avoided Lim's gaze. 'You know, you're the big hero here, Katt. If you didn't see something strange and started pursuing it, all four of them would get away with murder. I wonder how many other people have intentionally killed with their motor vehicles and just received fines and suspensions of licence. From now on, anyone who thinks about this will have to think twice.' He paused. 'Thanks to you.'

'Well, I'm just glad I could do my job.'

'Very well, I should say; very well.' He glanced at Katt, who was himself staring off into space. 'Is this your first murder case?' Katt nodded. 'First possible death penalty case too?' Katt nodded again.

'The first one is the most difficult. Except if you get one where you're not *really* sure, and then that one's even more difficult.' He then took a deep breath and stared into space himself. 'Are you vegetarian?'

Katt shook his head. 'No. I tried to be for a few years when I was at school. I was pretty good with it for awhile. But then KFC and Burger King beat out my grandfather's piety.'

'Well, that's good really. The officers who are vegetarian, they're the ones who usually have problems with death penalty cases. The rest of us get over it eventually.'

'That's good to hear,' Katt replied. But he kept seeing the torn look on Sondra Seow's face, the scared look on Ong's face, the confused look on Daniel Tay's. The only face that he could feel real, implacable contempt for was Axel Gersten's, sitting there in all its settled arrogance.

After an awkward stretch of silence, Lim stood and slapped the top of Katt's desk.

'Come on, partner – let's go out and have a celebration drink. We've got ourselves a big victory to celebrate here.'

Katt turned. 'Yeah, that's right. We do have a victory to celebrate, don't we?'

'Absolutely,' answered Lim, as he turned and headed towards the door. For several moments, Katt seemed trapped in his chair, unable to move. But then he stood up, nodded confidently and followed Lim out. And as he walked along, he felt, for maybe the first time, how well he fit into the space he was passing through.

Richard Lord is the author or co-author of over 20 published books and has edited or co-edited over two dozen volumes. His first full-length books were non-fiction titles, including *Culture Shock! Germany; Success in Business – Germany;* and *Insider's Frankfurt.* Among the books he's edited was *Crime Scene Singapore*, the prototype for the current *Crime Scene Asia* series.

For the last six years, Lord has been concentrating more and more on fiction, especially crime fiction. His short stories have appeared in five anthologies as well as in the now defunct Amazon Shorts program. One of his short stories, 'The Lost History of Shadows', was adapted as a mini-series for Singapore's Mediacorp television. This followed the adaptation of his earlier story, 'A Perfect Exit', as a one-hour TV film, also on Mediacorp.

His novel, *The Strangler's Waltz*, a murder mystery set in 1913 Vienna, is published by Monsoon Books. It is the first volume in a projected four-novel crime fiction series, *The Vienna Noir Quartet*.

Malaysia

THE CAT CITY CAPER

DAWN FARNHAM

'There's a museum'
　'Right.'
　'The place is called Cat.'
　'The museum?'
　'No; the place, the town.'
　'The town is called Cat?'
　'Well it's called Kuching, but it means Cat.'
　'Ker-ching means Cat?'
　'Not "Ker-ching" like in cash register. Kuching like in cat.
In Malay.'
　I stared at him. He saw my confusion.
　'In Malay. The language. Cat is Kuching. Sarawak.'
　'Zara Whack. Someone called Zara Whack?'
　'No, it's a state. In Malaysia.'
　'There's a state called Zara Whack?'

I was fairly new to the Orient, but this didn't sound right.

'Yeah. There's a museum.'

I felt my brain wilt. Just looking at Louis Chang could do that. He had one eye which spun lazily to the left and a cauliflower ear, both courtesy of his kick boxing days. We were of short acquaintance, but I'd realised early on that he was pathologically incapable of getting to the point unless he needed a beer which, fortunately, was generally early in the conversation.

He'd called me up.

'You need to get out of town.'

'Yeah,' I said, 'why?'

'Lulu's looking for you. Says you owe him money. Says you used another fence. He's not happy.'

I reflected on this a moment. We'd done a couple of small jobs together and he had screwed me, I knew it. On the last job I decided to cut him out and use a nice lady fence I'd met in a bar. Her name sounded like Kiddy Porn, but I liked her. Anyway, it wasn't honour amongst thieves, so what did I care. What was I, his mother?

'What am I, his mother?' I said to Louis.

Louis shrugged. 'Lulu wants an op.'

He blinked and his left eye rolled towards the door. My eyes narrowed. I was in the ladyboy capital of the world. Should I ask?

'Tonsils?'

'Dick. Cut it off. He needs the money.'

I stared at him.

'Wants a vag, you know. The dick. No use to him.'

'Well, well,' I said.

'You need to get out of town and you need dough. I got just the job.'

'Why does he want an op? He does a good job of screwing people over with his current dick.'

'You shouldn't say that. He's troubled.'

'Because of the dick thing. Right, I get it. We'll make up. When he's a girl, we'll go shopping.'

'That's nice. I'll tell him.'

'Her.'

'Right, when he's a she.'

I felt weary. Lulu on my tail was not a happy thought. I lit a cigarette.

'That'll kill you.'

'Not as fast as this conversation.'

'I need a drink. You wanna drink?'

Finally we were getting somewhere.

* * *

Cat City wasn't very big. A long brown river, a row of Chinese houses, colonial bits and pieces, too much honking traffic and hot, crowded drinking and eating holes. A litter of concrete cat statues and some ugly buildings, including the Hilton Hotel where I had a room. Louis had handed me a plane ticket and a thousand dollars and told me to go to the Irish Pub on the promenade and wait for some character named Bang Bang, a guy with a ponytail and a bone in his ear. He'd fill me in.

I'd toyed with absconding with the money, but he told me there was twenty thousand in it, split fifty-fifty between us. Louis was the go-to guy in Bangkok for all kinds of shady stuff.

There was a guy. A very rich guy. He wanted a statue which was in this private museum and he was happy to pay a lot of money for it. I should pay Bang Bang five hundred dollars and he would give me the low-down on the museum and help me get inside. I should get in, get the item, pass it to the rich guy's guy who would be waiting, take the ten thousand and get out of town.

Piece of cake, Louis said. No-one suspects a female burglar. It was my strong suit. And on this job, size mattered. I'd see.

This stuff about Lulu sounded dodgy. Lulu had a five o'clock shadow at midday and was built like a boxer. What sort of women would he make? The fool. He'd be the ugliest female in Asia. I'd worked hard to get into that billionaire's house and open the damn safe. That he might be pissed off was possible, however. It paid to be cautious. And this cat place, and this guy – the rich collector – I was interested. And I needed the money. The love of my life would be out in three months and would need funds.

An unusual profession for a woman, some may say. I hadn't intended to be a burglar, but you know how it is. My father had taught me everything I know, and he'd burgled on three continents.

When lover boy got banged up, I'd got out of Europe and wandered around Thailand for a while where I discovered that Bangkok was the most aptly named city in the world. I met up with Shamus Callaghan, loveable Irish crook and old friend of my father's. Shamus had put me in touch with Lulu and Louis and, voila, here we were.

Well, here I was, sitting in the Irish pub looking for a

guy with a bone in his ear. Two guys who looked like they'd recently had bones in their noses gave me the look. I ignored them. The waitress, dressed in a head scarf and a shamrock apron, came up, chewing gum. I ordered a sparkling water with a twist of lemon. No alcohol on the job, that was a rule.

'Stirred not shaken,' I said and smiled.

She stared at me, pencil poised, face flat, then turned and walked away.

'You Miss Gardner?'

His voice was a high whine. He was dark, tattooed, cross-eyed and had a long grey ponytail and a bone in his ear as big as my fist. What's with that? His nose was flat and his lower jaw jutted over the upper like a bulldog. Doubtless his mother loved him.

'Call me Ava,' I said and smiled.

I like to be charming if I can, and my alias is always an old movie star who anyone under the age of forty has never heard of. My real name is of no concern.

He smiled too, revealing a fence of gapped brown pickets and gums the colour of crushed grapes.

I felt a little sick and stared at the brown river for a while. When I looked back he was ogling my chest. For a female of my size, my tits are on the large side I suppose, but not abnormally so. Maybe, as his name suggested, Bang Bang had an overactive libido.

'Up here, soldier,' I said, pointing to my nose.

'Small,' he said. 'The entry is small.'

How could he know that!

He looked at my tits again. I finally got it.

'Let me worry about that.'

He revealed the wine gums and yellow pickets again, then grimaced.

'Got my money?'

I handed over half the five hundred.

'Rest when I'm done,' I said.

'Sure.' He grimaced again. 'Toothache,' he whined.

'Surprising,' I said. 'OK, fill me in.'

* * *

The museum was on a side street in an old house in Chinatown. It was devoted to the unique artefacts of the head hunters of Borneo and cats. Bang Bang showed me a map of the house conspiratorially, his breath stinkier than an orang-utan's armpit. He would show me the way to the house, to the small window on the second floor which he had left unlatched and from which he had loosened two bars. I was to gain access through this, walk to the ground floor and take the item, a wooden black-and-gold, lacquered cat, then exit the way I'd come.

Sounded so easy, I was wary.

'No alarms, lasers, bells ringing in police stations far away?'

He shook his head. 'No.'

'So why do you need me? You could do it yourself. Anyone could do it.'

'No, the window is small, I told you. But maybe your, you know …'

'Right, I told you don't worry about that.'

'And at night four valuable exhibits are put in a safe. The

cat is one of them.'

'OK, I see. Describe the safe.'

From his pocket, he produced a picture. It was a good safe. Would take some time, but there is no safe in the world which a good cracker can't break.

'Why does the guy want this cat?'

He shrugged.

'Dunno. It's the ugliest cat I've ever seen. Big fat belly, mean little eyes.'

If there's one thing I know, it's that there is no explaining what drives collectors. My father had made – and lost – a fortune because of the compulsive desires of collectors.

'I'll take a walk around the place tomorrow when it's open, get my bearings. We'll do it tomorrow night.'

Bang Bang nodded.

'Tomorrow' was Saturday. The museum would be shut all day Sunday. Time for me to get out of Cat City before it was even discovered.

* * *

I took a tour of the museum the next morning. The card next to the cat told me it was a totem of the native people of somewhere, used to give the evil eye to their enemies. It was on loan with thanks to Abdul Someone or Other. Bang Bang was right: it was an ugly thing. It was about a foot high and eight inches wide at its belly. It didn't look heavy. A standard bag would carry it out. I reckoned on an hour.

Actually, it took two. I strapped down the offending bits of myself which might be likely to catch on anything and slid through the window, no trouble. Down to the room with the safe. The lock on that door took thirty seconds, though the safe was recalcitrant. But there's no-one more patient than a safecracker, and the last click fell after an hour. I flashed my torch and found myself staring at a shrunken head. That gave me a bit of a turn. The cat was heavier than I'd thought, solid wood with a heavy gold base, but all in all, I was pleased with the job.

Back in the hotel room, I gave Bang Bang the rest of his dough. A man would be here at midnight, he said, take the cat and give me the money. I put the cat on the desk. It really was an ugly thing. Why on earth would anyone want to pay twenty thousand for it? Maybe the gold base was worth more than I thought. I examined it a little closer, but it didn't get any better. Well, what did I care? I ordered room service and took a shower. Now where would I go to spend my ten thousand bucks?

I was thinking fondly of Louis Chang when there was a knock at the door. Ah, just the thing, poached salmon and a beer. I threw a towel over the cat, opened the door and found myself flying across the carpet. My head made contact with the leg of the desk and I saw stars.

'You bitch,' Lulu snarled.

'How the hell ... ?' I began scrambling to find my feet, shaking off the stars. It didn't entirely work, and before I could say another word, Lulu had picked me up and thrown me onto the bed. At least it was a soft landing.

My brain was whirling. How on earth was I to get out of this?

'Lulu, calm down. We can work something out. Louis told

me about your ... problem.'

To my astonishment, Lulu sat down on the chair at the desk and stared at me. Two fat tears ran down his face.

'You don't know. It's been so hard.'

'You want to be a girl, I get it.'

He sobbed, his massive shoulders heaving. He had the biceps of a prize fighter and thighs to match. His ears alone were bigger than my hands.

'Have you thought this through, Lulu? High heels are hell.'

How could I get rid of him before the collector got here. I was gonna have to share the money. No; correction: I was gonna have to give him the money. I started to get pissed off. I rubbed my neck where it had come into contact with teak.

He looked at me. Perhaps my tone was a touch more sarcastic than I'd intended. His girlish side disappeared.

'You got a job here. Louis said five thousand. I want it.'

He made a fist. My cockiness disappeared. Damn Louis Chang, double-crossing bastard. Even double-crossing the double-cross.

'Now Lulu, we girls have to stick together.'

I got off the bed, feeling more secure on my feet. He rose.

'You laughing at me?'

'No, no, Lulu.'

'You're laughing at me, you bitch.'

He lunged and I ducked. I picked up the towel and threw it at him. I grabbed the cat. If I could get out of the room, I'd find Bang Bang and maybe this situation would sort itself out somehow or other.

But Lulu must have read my mind. He came for me. I knew he would do me some serious harm and without any further thought, I lofted the cat and threw it at his head. The heavy metal bottom landed with a crunch right on his temple and he went down like a stone. I could hardly believe it. He was out cold, but I knew it might not be for long.

I grabbed my bag, threw a few things in, including my clutch of passports and the money. I stepped over Lulu and looked for the cat. To my horror, I realised it was broken. The head had come off and rolled under the bed.

I got down on my hands and knees. How long did I have before that brute on the floor woke up? And now the damn cat was broken. I found the head and went for the body. Maybe the guy wouldn't mind. I felt my heart sink. Maybe Lulu would be named Miss Thailand.

That's when I saw it. A flash. Inside the body of the cat. That's when I realised that the head was meant to come off the cat and the body was hollow. Another flash. I put my hand inside and out they came in a neat plastic packet.

Diamonds! Must have been two hundred pure white diamonds. I sat back on my haunches. No wonder the guy wanted this ugly statue. It was the hiding place for some previous theft, parked in the museum until the heat died down. Whatever! Didn't matter how they'd got there or why, here they were, sparkling in my little hand, a million dollars in diamonds. With a fence, I'd still be sweet with half.

Lulu emitted a low groan and rolled onto his side.

In a flash, I pocketed the diamonds, threw my bag into the wardrobe and screwed the head back onto the cat.

I wet a towel and put it to his brow.

'Sorry, Lulu. You scared me. Look, I admit I was wrong.'

Lulu sat and narrowed his eyes, then groaned again.

'I'll make it up to you. Call it quits.'

I handed the cat to him.

'The guy will be here at midnight. Louis is a liar. You should beat him up. Hell, beat 'em all up. It's twenty-five thousand big ones. Don't take less. I feel bad knowing what you need it for.'

Lulu stared at me in amazement. I began to throw clothes into my suitcase.

'Use my room, take a bath. The salts are lavender. You'll like them.'

Lulu stood up. *Uh oh*, I thought as he came towards me.

But he was crying again and pulled me into a bear hug.

'Thank you, thank you. I'm sorry I scared you. It's the hormones. I have to take them and they make me crazy."

I withdrew and patted him on the cheek.

'Welcome to my world.'

He thought that was funny. We both laughed. We were BFF.

I gathered my things. The last I saw of him, he was cradling the cat and sobbing like a baby.

* * *

The taxi sped through the night. A call rang out on the air which smelled of heat and durian. Cat City. I liked it. I settled back.

I suspected Louis knew about the diamonds, sent me to do the safe-cracking, but didn't want to pay out and sent Lulu to sort me out. Greedy, greedy. By the time he found out, I'd be back in Europe. There was a guy in Amsterdam I knew.

The taxi turned into the airport.

With any luck, they'd pin it all on Lulu. He'd finally get his wish. Somebody would have his balls.

Dawn Farnham's writing is wide-ranging and includes novels, short stories, children's books, plays and screenplays.

She is author of The Straits Quartet, a four-part series of historical novels set in 19th-century Singapore and *A Crowd of Twisted Things*, a woman's search for her missing child set against the background of the Maria Hertogh race riots of 1950s Singapore, all published by Monsoon Books.

As part of newly formed Western Australia-based Tempest Productions, she is working on various projects including a rock/art documentary, short film scripts and a television series.

Currently, she is also writing a children's chapter book about the friendship of three children from very different backgrounds in 1900s Perth and researching a *Vanity Fair*-type novel about a ruthless young woman seeking her fortune in 1850s Australia.

She is also working on a play – a satire of the arts scene in Perth – which hopes to take a humorous and gentle dig at the cultural life of the world's most isolated city.

Philippines

ON A WET DAY
YOU CAN LIVE FOREVER

CHARLSON ONG

What is with rain that follows me around like a sick dog looking for some place to die? It was clear skies when we left the station. Earlier it was even bright and summery, now it's all wet and gloom. December drizzles are like homeless sots: spineless and odious, begging for some holiday freebie, out of season, out of reason.

Global warming, they say. Everything's out of whack: typhoons in February, crazy heat in August, rain in December. The glaciers are melting, seas are rising … the damn sky is falling. *We'll have snow in these parts before you know it*, says Marcos, who is our main man in Forensics but has a minor as well in Meteorology – from the UP, no less. Who on earth takes up Meteorology, Marcos? I'm sure you partied every night with Misses Low Pressure Area and Tropical Depression.

And what do you call your Fraternity: Alpha Wrong Tornado?

Right, but Marcos' father was a weather forecaster who later sold insurance. That says what sort of son Marcos is. You don't get that kind of children any more. My own daughter's been in Singapore for the past two years designing shop windows; joined her mom, Connie, my-ex, who's been counting stop lights or something – works for the traffic bureau. Not an e-mail or text message in months, as if the old man's just so much cyber-nuisance.

In any case, I say to Marcos: You were two decades too early for CNN. When I was a kid, it was just this Cebuano guy Amado Pineda on Channel 7 in barong and umbrella. But he was the real thing, genuine forecaster, PhD. None of these razzle-dazzle blowhards with their touch screens and Google maps.

And genuine article too, Dr Marcos Panelos. With his flashlight, and tweezers and dilators, he can give you the low-down on any corpse in ten minutes tops. And that's why I like dragging him along – for the price of a Johnny Walker Black – to important crime scenes for an on-site appraisal of the evidence before it may be degraded en route to crime lab. The way some of these orderlies handle corpses, I'd bet they moonlight in slaughterhouses. I suspect, too, that Marcos is psychic and that he communes, perhaps subconsciously, with the spirit of the newly expired and that makes his on-site deductions uncanny. I've never said this to him though, not even in jest. I'm not sure if he believes in an afterlife after what he's seen of the dead, and I'm wary of freaking him out.

Little Baguio, San Juan. I hadn't been in these parts since leaving with my family at 14, save when driving through Ortigas Avenue or occasionally checking out the Green Hills Shopping Center for cheap electronics knock-offs.

There wasn't much of a Green Hills subdivision when I was a boy. Little Baguio was mostly grassland and scrub back then. It was always hilly and the topography likely earned the place its moniker. Back when it took forever to get to the real Baguio, and San Juan was still 'country' – over an hour's drive from downtown Manila – the Olmedos, and Manzanos, and Samaniegos built vacation homes of hard wood and concrete with small gardens and duck ponds out here that old folks described as 'colonial.'

My mom used to walk to six o'clock mass at the Mary the Queen parish church every evening with a scion of a former President, or so she recalled. In time, the vacation homes were abandoned and we neighbourhood kids grew up thinking of them as haunted or lairs of *dwende* and *kapre* – dwarfs and tree demons. Then there were all those stories about people killed or buried hereabout during the Japanese occupation. I guess it was partly our parents' way of keeping us from roaming too far or too late into the *talahib*. But, really, who doesn't believe in ghosts? After all, there were the occasional skulls and bones dug up and, once, a fairly fresh hand.

They're mostly gone now, the old houses, as well as our rented home, replaced by high rises and condos.

We moved here in 1959, when San Juan was still part of Rizal province rather than Metro Manila and I was a toddler. We moved into a two-storey apartment block, supposedly owned by the country's boxing hero of the day – the 'Flash' Elorde. Both my parents were part-Chinese and accountants. My dad – Herminio Lantad, Sr. – kept books for a lumber store in Binondo. My mom, Lucia Dy-liaco, wanted a Catholic education for me, their first and (as it turned out) only son, but wanted me to learn to read and write Chinese as well. So when the Jesuits moved their Xavier School from Echague, Manila, to seven hectares of boondocks in San Juan, we followed suit. In time, more families joined us – as the Immaculate Concepcion Academy all-girls' school sat a block across from Xavier. And within two decades, the Ortigas' Green Hills gated subdivision had sprung up with its mansions and shopping centre and bowling lanes and another boys' school – La Salle Green Hills – with whose denizens we rumbled over girls or football or just for the heck of it.

In my boyhood though, Little Baguio was middle-class residential. My late granny used to call it 'barbarian town', because of the Chinese *mestiza* ladies who played mahjong without let-up as well as a slew of 'kept women' and 'second families'.

Our one miserly Chinese *sari-sari* storekeeper and vegetable-seller, bald and wiry, gossiped like an old crone but he showed up at our place one day, in black suit and tie, to say that he was going home to China for his son's wedding. It was the first time anyone had thought of him as a family man. He came back with gifts of tea and lychees. Shortly after he returned from China, he went missing. A week later, an awful smell emanated from his room. When the neighbours broke in, they found him stabbed to death many times over, along with his dog, an abandoned terrier he had rescued years earlier.

It was the first murder in our neighbourhood since anyone could remember. The cops came and the next day, we found out his full name in the papers: Pablo Lao. He had lived alone in Little Baguio for the past twenty-some years, the last six with his dog. He had lately employed a young man to do odd chores who had also gone missing.

Robbery was the likely motive, but why thirty stab wounds? Why the ghastliness? No one ever found out.

The cops had no leads and no interest in pursuing the case. Pablo had no family in the Philippines. The Lao surname association arranged a cremation; there was not even a wake. I can't say even now whether or not that was the time I thought of becoming a cop. I must have been eight or nine, but I began to feel that something had gone wrong with the world that must be made right.

But Little Baguio had its share of celebrity, too. In the late 1960s, we had for town mayor of San Juan an action movie star who would someday become Philippine president. He lived, with his second wife, in a big house around three blocks uphill from our place and reportedly pissed on the shoes of town cops when soused. And for our neighbour, we had another movie star, a romantic one, Vic Moreno, recently separated from his actress wife. He would be godfather to many of the neighbourhood kids for the year or so that he stayed in Little Baguio.

Still what I remember best about San Juan were the 'wet days'. June 24, the feast of John the Baptist (who is the patron saint of San Juan) was off-limits to anyone averse to being bathed by exultant residents. At crack of dawn, we were all out in the streets with pails and *tabo* in hand, throwing water at each other as well as passing cars and jeepneys. In time, pails and *tabo* would be replaced by garden hoses that neighbours trained on each other.

And then, in my twelfth year, trouble erupted as some outsider threw dank *estero* water up the miniskirt of a pretty lass leaving for work. Her grandfather ran down the street with his .38 cal and blew away the offender. That, I reckon, marked the end of San Juan as a small town. St. John's Day would never again be the same. Suddenly, we seemed to be among strangers with sinister designs and the old rules no longer held. It was less than two years since Pablo's murder.

That was more or less what I was trying to tell Marcos as we drove through the rain. But Marcos, as always, was more interested in the crime page of the tabloid he read religiously: Headless corpse in overcoat found near Rizal Monument.

The house, one I remember well from my boyhood, sits on a hilly incline. It was 'old' even when I was a boy; some 160 sq. meters, but dubbed 'American' rather than 'Spanish': single storey with carved nymph on red brick walls, tiled porch and large windows. Old timers called it 'La Azotea'.

It was rumoured that the first owner murdered his wife in bed and few residents stayed long despite the low rent. When I was in high school, a stern middle-aged bachelorette, Ms Covar, who worked as a cashier in our school, rented the place and took in our librarian, Ms Diana, as boarder.

After some months, Ms Covar went away and Ms Diana stayed on for another semester before she too went away. In the 1990s, a movie starlet lived here and hanged herself one day. It was always unclear who owned the property.

I feel goose bumps all over as we enter the premises – the first time I've been here in nearly forty years – and notice that not much has changed. 'They don't build houses like these anymore,' I whisper. Marcos snorts.

The San Juan Police are already on hand, dusting for prints, talking to a witness – the victim's house help – taking photos. I flash my badge. 'Inspector Jun Lantad, Narcotics Division,' I say to the officer in charge. He nods: Superintendent Ben Lizares, San Juan PD.

It's really their turf, their crime. But Headquarters had called up Narcotics earlier to request a look-see. Intelligence suspects that the deceased, Isabel Villa, a sometime ramp model and former mistress to suspected drug lord Benito Saludar (a.k.a. Benny Lim, a.k.a. Lam Bien So), had been done in. This after she had sent feelers to testify against Saludar. If her death was drug-related, then we might have enough to go after Saludar. That, anyway, was the explanation of my boss, Col. Samson Sotto, even as I insisted that it was a matter for Homicide. 'Get your ass over there, Lantad,' Sotto barked, 'and take that nut case Panelos with you.'

'Any sign of foul play?' I ask Lizares. He shrugs. 'Your turn,' he says, indicating the deceased. One big family, we cops are.

Marcos peers at the body, pokes the eyes and lips, then takes out his stethoscope to listen to something inside the chest, the abdomen.

I'm dumfounded. I've never seen him do such a thing. 'What?' I ask him after minutes. He smirks, shakes his head and walks away. 'Well?' I insist.

'Probably not your case,' he says and lights up.

'Don't contaminate the crime scene,' I say. He leaves the house and I follow, still confounded.

'That shit will kill you,' I say. I've quit smoking since expelling a glob of brackish spunk months ago. Quit the *shabu* too. I'd used a bit of it in the beginning just to learn how to better deal with junkies, but it started to grow on me and I began using more and more until Connie kicked me out. I went cold turkey.

'No drugs,' Marcos says. 'My best bet is aneurysm. She might have burst a brain vessel, but I can't be sure till we cut her up at the barn.' I feel strange relief and walk back in. Last time I was here, I was 14 and pining to get laid. I had walked Ms Diana Castro home, carrying her stuff. She had been librarian for a month, replacing old Mrs Yap, who retired.

Our newfangled Learning Resource Center (LRC) was air-conditioned, and the school was experimenting with an 'Individualized Instruction' method, using our batch as guinea pig, which meant lots of 'self-study' time that we freshmen mostly spent at the LRC talking shit and ogling Ms Diana.

She was 24, a pretty *morena*, around 5 ft. 4, with a pert nose and full lips. I think it was the lips that got our tails wagging. She smiled at our insipid jokes and told us to hush. 'I'll lose my job,' she said, as some six of us fluttered about her, and her voice sounded like what ice cream soda might taste with a sip of beer.

Vincent Uy produced the 'magic mirror' that had supposedly shown him every underwear of every miniskirted teacher worth espying on. We parked ourselves across from her desk and pretended to read.

Then she got up and hobbled towards a bookshelf. At

first, I thought she had a bad sprain. Then we all saw perhaps the biggest downer of our young lives: she had only one good leg, a stunner, but her right one was thin as a twelve-year-old child's. Ms Diana was a polio victim.

There was an embarrassed, maybe melancholic, silence among us. We didn't know what to say. We knew it was awful to laugh, but someone did, perhaps just to relieve the tension. Then everyone left.

Until today, I can't well describe that moment. It was like a light had gone on inside my head that I could never turn off, even at night, even when I go to sleep. 'She was like this damselfly, on her last days, flitting on a broken wing,' I said to Connie once, in later years. 'Go take out the trash,' she replied. 'That shit will kill you.'

While my mates stopped floating about Ms Diana, I was strangely more attracted to her. They taunted me no end. My neighbour, James Wong, whose family later moved to Canada, even brought a sex doll to school one day to show me what was what. But I didn't care.

She was bright, Ms Diana. She knew stuff, not just librarian stuff but real-life stuff. She bought Vendo cups of grasshoppers and dragonflies from the grade school kids. Our football field always had loads of these insects flitting about and we caught them, too, as kids. James Wong was champ. He could fill a cup in thirty minutes of recess. I could hardly nab one; didn't have the hand-eye coordination and quickness. I was never good at these things. But we didn't have much to do with our catch – James' catch that is – and the poor slobs often just died on us or were set free. Now the tykes could sell to Ms Diana: one peso per insect, two for a damselfly.

'What do you do with them?' I asked.

'Watch them die,' she said, 'then mount them.' She showed me her picture books and collection of dead insects: beetles, grasshoppers, dragonflies, butterflies and moths.

She was an amateur entomologist. Took up Biology in college. 'I wanted to be a doctor, a surgeon,' she said.

'So why are you here?'

She shrugged; shit happens.

Dragonflies are ancient by seven weeks. By that time, if they've survived predators, they would have each lived two lives – as larvae and adult – mated, and produced offspring. Then they die.

'Short life,' I said.

'But they've been around for 300 million years,' she said. 'Can you imagine that?

'No.'

'They were here before the dinosaurs. They'll be here after we're long gone.'

'Really?'

'Yes, dragonflies are forever.'

Then she showed me the amber. There were pieces shaped like hearts, and livers and horns. Some were no bigger than my toenail, others the size of a pinball. 'I found this one in a cave in Montalban,' she said. It reminded me of a toad.

'Flowers aren't defenceless,' Ms Diana explained. 'Sometimes when an insect, a dragonfly, perhaps, alights on a petal, it secretes a sticky resin that traps the insect and encases it. In time, they become amber. So who knows what these things contain? A prehistoric flea perhaps,' she said, holding up the amber to my eyes.

'Fascinating,' I whispered.

'So what did we learn today?' she asked.

I shrugged. 'Never throw away stuff?'

She smiled. 'Never trust a flower.' She then pressed a finger on the tip of my nose and made my day.

It would be many years later, while watching *Jurassic Park*, that I got the drift of Ms Diana's lesson to me that day, the year Martial Law cut short the school term.

I insisted on walking her home to La Azotea, which was three blocks from school. There were some toughies around the corner, and the last stretch was uphill. I could imagine Ms Diana's difficulties and offered to carry the books she often brought home to read.

The first few times she wouldn't let me in, wary of Ms Covar. 'She doesn't like people entering her home,' Ms Diana said.

'Why, how many corpses has she got in there?' I asked in jest, but Ms Diana turned serious: 'Don't say such things.'

'I'm sorry,' I whispered.

But one evening, she did ask me in because I'd carried a huge pile, and Ms Covar was away, and perhaps there was a drizzle. Ms Diana opened a bottle of beer and offered me one.

'I know you guys drink,' she said. I would've never guessed she did. The beer, in fact, turned out to be from Ms Covar's stash.

'So what are they calling you these days?' she asked. 'Librarian's pet? Horny dog?'

I swallowed hard.

'I know how it is,' she went on. Something had changed as she lounged on the sofa. 'I heard you guys laughing that day,' she said.

My tongue was stone. 'They always do,' she whispered, staring at me.

'I'm sorry,' I said.

'So what happened when you saw the Pinocchio leg?' she asked, then curled an upraised finger when I said nothing. I was stunned and looked down, cradling my beer.

'So how old are you, anyway?'

'Fourteen.'

'You know what I did at fourteen?' I shook my head. Her eyes seemed glazed.

'He taunted me since we were small,' she said. 'I couldn't run so I was always the *It*. He would tie me up and roll me inside a barrel. Once he stripped me and pushed me into a cold river. I never told. But the day I turned fourteen, when he came to my party, I took a bat and slugged it across his head. Then they all went away and I was rid of them; forever.'

The silence between us was a wall of bad air.

'So what is it you want?' she asked finally. I had no answer. Seconds later, her laughter collapsed the silence.

'I got you, didn't I?' she asked, vibrant again, winsome.

'Another bottle, she asked? I think I deserve one more,' she said, 'for all the rent that old maid charges'.

She started to get up. I moved instinctively to help, but she waived me away stiffly and I backed off. Still I followed her to the kitchen, trying to be useful. I might have brushed her nape as she reached for the refrigerator door and she suddenly turned on me with a knife.

'Stop it!' she shouted, and I felt my balls in my throat. I froze.

She quickly turned away and laid down the knife. I thought she was shaking but didn't dare touch her. She breathed deeply. I feared she might be having an asthma attack.

'I'm sorry,' she whispered, 'so sorry.' I felt cold sweat break out. She half-turned to me.

'You're too young,' she whispered, 'Too young ... Go away now... Go away.' And I did.

We left Little Baguio before the new school year started. My father had lost his job in Binondo and got a new one in, of all places, Baguio. But I always suspected that he wanted another, a safer, place for me.

I spent the rest of my high school years up there and came back to Manila for college, taking up Criminology to my parents' utter disappointment. The memory of Ms Diana slowly faded, but I'd sometimes wake up in the middle of night and think of dead dragonflies.

Now I call up Marcos. 'Something's amiss.'

'You know what time it is?' he asks.

'Two a.m.; so what?'

'So you're bothering my wife.'

'You have no wife,' I say.

'Of course, I have,' he snipes back. 'Some nights.'

'We didn't check out the shed,' I say.

'There is no shed,' he says.

'Yes there is ... there was. I remember now. I walked into it once, and I saw a chainsaw. She said Ms Covar had borrowed it to have the mango tree felled. She wanted more space in the yard. But the tree's still there. I bet it hasn't been bothered with in forty years.

'She even showed me how to use the chainsaw. How did she know how to use a darn chainsaw?'

'What on earth are you talking about? What chainsaw? What tree? Who is Ms Covar? And why is any of this my problem?' Marcos shouts.

'Ms Covar never came back,' I say. 'Ms Diana stayed on for the rest of the semester, then she resigned.

'One day I was called to the Principal's office and there was this guy who asked me questions about Ms Diana: What did she say? What did she read? Did she drink? Do drugs? Who were her friends? Did she talk about her family? Did she say she was from Davao? Did she like Ms Covar? Was there anything strange about her? What was the extent of your relationship? What did you do at her boarding place?

'She's an entomologist,' that was all I said. 'But he was a cop. I'll bet my life that joker was a cop. I asked him, but he wouldn't let on.'

Marcos hangs up.

I go back to La Azotea early in the morning. The place is still off-limits to anyone but the police. Marcos was right: there is no shed. Had I imagined it? No. I've finally turned off the light inside my head and see everything clearly.

I hear barking and see a mongrel chasing away a cat. Something white is sticking out of the ground. I call headquarters for diggers.

There was a hand, then a tibia, then a skull and fragments of spine. Forty-five to fifty, female,' I say to Brix, the Forensics intern. Marcos had refused to come. He looks at the bones. then at me.

'You psychic?' he asks.

I smile. 'Yes, I think so.'

I dig up files on several Diana Castros, but none of them match the Ms Diana I knew. She might have used an alias in Manila, and I can't trace anything back to Davao. The search on Ms Anita Covar also leads to a dead end.

Marcos tells me that my hunch about the Little Baguio bones are spot on, but it's near impossible now to say whom they belong to if they're too old. We don't have the data to match. Still, who knows, we might be able to use them to pin down Saludar.

But, here's the rub: there are traces of arsenic on the bones, and amber lodged in one of the ribs.

'She targeted loners,' I say. 'If no one is looking, then no one is missing,' I tell Marcos. 'That's why she let me go ... that night. I wonder how many victims she had?'

'Give me a break, Lantad,' Marcos says. 'The woman pulls a knife at your horny 14-year-old dick and she's a serial killer? A butcher lady? You're pathetic!'

'You know the dead, Marcos,' I say. 'I know the living.'

'You know bullshit,' he says.

And he's probably right, just like the time he talked about facts and causes.

'Facts I deal with,' he said, 'causes are the stories you make up to draw a pay check.'

'OK, OK, Marcos. But I never told you how I got a letter shortly before we left Little Baguio. There was a piece of amber inside, the one she found in Montalban, and a note:

'Thanks for being a friend. When you grow older, things will seem clearer. Think well of me.'

'And I do, Marcos. I think well of her, really. But I think I was the one who laughed that day.'

'I didn't mean to, but I did,' I tell Connie on the mobile.

'Don't start, Jun,' she whispers, and shuts off her phone.

But the stuff is beginning to work on me, so I go outside for some fresh air and it is a wet day in Little Baguio. And we're all soaked to the bone with our pails, and *tabo* and garden hoses. My father's in his boxers having a ball; he didn't die of a heart attack in Burnham Park at 58. And my mother's in her raincoat dowsing our chow dog, Tiger, she didn't pass away in her sleep at 75.

And there's Vic Moreno, not movie actor-like, but frolicking with his many *inaanak*, he didn't die in a car crash at 50. And Pablo Lao's there too, bald and skinny, shooing everyone away from his vegetable cart. And Ms Covar, still demure, but letting her hair down this one day in the year. 'It's the only day she bathes,' James Wong shouts into my ears. He didn't get killed as a war correspondent in Iraq.

Then I see her, at last: Ms Diana, on her one good leg, a stunner, training a hose at me and I almost laugh, but manage to stop myself this time.

I know I must live forever before this shit kills me.

Charlson Ong has published three collections of short fiction: *Men of the East and Other Stories*; *Woman of Am Kaw and other stories*, *Conversion and other Fictions* as well as three novels: *An Embarrassment of Riches*;

Banyaga, A Song of War; *Blue Angel/ White Shadow*. He has won prizes from the Carlos Palanca Memorial Awards, the Philippines Free Press, Philippines Graphic, Asiaweek, (Philippines) National Book Awards (for short fiction and the novel), the Philippines Centennial Literary Competition. He was also given the Southeast Asia (SEA) Write Award in 2012.

India

THE CASE OF THE TOO MANY FINGERPRINTS

ABHA IYENGAR

Inspector Monty stood in front of the mirror, proudly surveying himself. At forty, he still cut a natty figure. Apart from a slight widening of the girth, which disappeared when he sucked his stomach in, he thought he looked good.

His mobile, lying on the bedside table, rang. He lunged for it like a young schoolboy. His eagerness was evident; this was because he knew the call was from his lady love, police officer Maya. He called her his Maya *Memsahib*. Both of them worked together in the Crime Branch. He had been wooing her for several years, but she refused to marry him, saying that she prized her independence.

Her voice was urgent. 'Monty,' she said, 'come quickly to 10, Jordan Hill. A murder has been committed. I'll meet you there.' She disconnected before he could question her further.

Monty revved up his bike. Jordan Hill was quite far from where he lived, so he decided to speed up a bit.

* * *

Jordan Hill was a posh area, a secluded lane of twelve houses. Number 10 was a two-storey house, with vines climbing its sides, and lush, well-tended lawns. The red-tiled roof and rough grey exterior finish of the house aimed to give it a rustic look. However, it spoke of money well spent. The heavy, wooden front door was now ajar.

Monty could see Maya's blue Maruti 800 parked outside. He parked his bike next to her car, and felt his heart lurch at the sight of such togetherness. He squared his shoulders with pride and sauntered in with a masterful air. Maya met him in the hallway, and led him to the kitchen, where the body of an old man, in a once-white kurta-pyjama, lay in a pool of blood. Nothing had been touched. By his side lay a revolver, obviously the murder weapon.

He could hear women crying. Maya walked with him into the living room, where an old lady was sitting on the watered silk sofa, sobbing quietly. A middle-aged, plumpish maid, dark of skin and wearing a nylon sari of indeterminate print, cowered in one corner on her haunches. Tears coursed down her fat cheeks. A teenaged girl, slim and wheatish-complexioned, was sitting with her arms wrapped tightly around the plump woman. She was sobbing incoherently.

Inspector Monty was a bit perturbed by this emotional scene. Maya touched his arm reassuringly. He straightened up and adopted a more official demeanour. On his entrance, the women in the room tried to wipe their tears.

Monty sat on the chair opposite the old lady. Maya took one of the other sofa chairs. The plump woman got up and stood in the corner with the slim girl close to her, holding onto her arm. Both of them seemed to be supporting each other.

Monty waited for someone to speak. Someone would break the silence.

The old lady spoke. 'Inspector, that man lying there is my husband, Colonel Verma.'

She broke out in sobs again. 'She ... killed him.' She pointed an accusing finger at the plump woman.

Maya said quietly to Monty, 'That is their maid, Vandana. And next to her is her daughter, Sunita.'

Vandana, cowering in the corner, refused to say anything, and kept sobbing into the frayed end of her sari. Her daughter stood protectively next to her.

Monty looked at Mrs Verma. 'What makes you say that, madam?' he enquired.

'She's admitted it,' the old lady replied.

Monty looked at Vandana now. 'You killed the Colonel?'

Vandana shook her head, as if to say 'Yes'.

'Did you kill the Sahib, Vandana?' Maya asked her gently.

'Yes, madam,' Vandana sobbed.

'What for?'

'He was trying to ... my daughter, Sunita,' she said.

'What?'

'In the night ... in the kitchen ... I came to turn off the kitchen light, I thought I'd left it on by mistake.' She stopped talking, emotion overtaking her.

'And …?' prompted Maya.

'Sahib was holding Sunita against the wall in a compromising position. I looked at my daughter's eyes; she was facing me. I could not stand it. I rushed to the living room, took out Sahib's revolver, and shot him!' She was sobbing again.

Monty watched her face as she talked to Maya. Monty realized that her tears were for her daughter, not for having shot the Colonel.

The young girl was quiet. Maya looked at her watch. Monty said they were taking Vandana away to the police station for further questioning.

'I'll take care of Sunita,' said Mrs Verma to Vandana suddenly. Monty's moustache twitched once. When this happened, Monty knew that something was not right. It was not normal for a person to offer to look after the child of her husband's murderer.

Maya told Mrs Verma and Sunita to stay in. They were not to touch anything, and would be questioned again later. Still sobbing, Vandana followed Monty and Maya out.

* * *

The forensic report came in the next morning. The old man had been shot from the back. There were three sets of fingerprints on the revolver: two were most likely female, one male! One set of prints matched Vandana's, but the other two? Monty called Maya, and they decided to meet at 10 Jordan Hill again, to continue their interrogation.

Referring to the forensic report findings, Maya told Monty,

'Current science can only determine the high probability of one gender or the other.' She emphasized 'high probability', her face extremely serious. 'So we can't be too gender conscious here.'

Monty nodded and rang the bell.

'Good morning, Sunita,' said Monty to the young girl as she opened the door for them. She looked dishevelled and frail, with dark patches under her eyes.

'How's my mother?' she asked, sounding concerned and unhappy.

Maya said, 'She's fine, Sunita. Where is Mrs Verma?'

'Memsahib is resting. She doesn't wish to be disturbed,' Sunita answered.

'So we'll just come in and wait awhile,' said Monty, and they walked in.

Sunita stood quietly in the middle of the living room. She was a pretty girl, with the delicacy of newly blossoming youth. She must have been barely fourteen.

'Sit down,' said Maya; Sunita sat on the floor.

'I am going to ask you a few questions, Sunita. Don't be afraid,' said Maya. Head down, Sunita nodded.

'Can you tell us what happened that night?' asked Maya.

'My mother has already told you.'

'We want to hear it from you,' Maya said gently.

Sunita began her story. Her mother, a widow, had been employed at Colonel Verma's for over five years now. Sunita had grown up here, and had begun helping her mother in the household chores. Recently, the Colonel had started making amorous advances towards her. She had at first ignored it, but later complained to her mother. They had decided that they would leave the job and find some other place for work. Her mother had been asking around. And then that night ...

Sunita continued. 'I had gone to the kitchen to fetch myself a glass of water. The Colonel Sahib also came into the kitchen. I stepped aside to let him open the fridge. Instead, he caught hold of my arm and pulled me towards him. When I tried to resist, he pushed me against the wall and began kissing me. It was *Bhaiya* ...'

She had begun crying now and was trying to wipe her tears away with the back of her hands, leaving dirt marks on her soft cheeks. Monty noticed that her fingers were long, the hands delicate, and the skin so fine that the bones almost shone through. It would have been very easy to overpower this girl.

He returned to the present. '*Bhaiya?*' Had the girl said 'Bhaiya'?

Maya was already asking Sunita, 'Who is this *Bhaiya*? Was there someone else in the house? Tell me, girl.' Her voice had a steely ring to it.

Sunita's hands flew to her face in despair. 'Oh no!' she said. 'It is nothing. The words just came out of my mouth.'

'Who is *Bhaiya?*' Maya's voice was firm.

'*Bhaiya* ... he is Raj *Bhaiya*, Sahib's son.'

'He was here that night?'

'Yes.' Sunita's voice was a whisper.

'And ... he saved you?'

'No, no ...'

Monty shot a volley of questions at the girl. 'He killed Colonel Verma? Where is he now? Why was he not here when we arrived?'

Sunita answered, 'I don't *know* who killed Sahib. I was

trying my best to push him away, pleading with him. I was not even aware that there were other people in the room. All I know was that I heard a shot, and before I knew it, Sahib was dead at my feet. My mother, the *memsahib* and *Bhaiya* were at the door. The gun was lying on the floor. My mother says she has killed him, but I know she is innocent. I do not know where *Bhaiya* is. Mrs Verma sent him away to some farm in Ludhiana.'

Sunita broke down. 'Please help my mother. I don't know who killed Sahib … I don't know …'

The girl was becoming incoherent. It was useless questioning her any further.

* * *

The Golden Egg Farm in Ludhiana was vast acres of land with a large sprawling bungalow, a swimming pool, tennis courts, rare flowers and well-manicured lawns where the clipped hedges had a disciplined look. Raj Verma was a slim, long-haired boy who sported a diamond in his ear and was dressed in blue jeans and a tee shirt. When Inspector Monty and Maya introduced themselves, his face registered shock, but he recovered soon enough.

'So what brings both of you so far from your home turf?' he asked.

Whatever brought you here, my dear, Maya felt like saying. She bit her tongue.

He introduced them to his friend, Ravi – a tall, well-built young man who twirled his moustache as he stood there, an intimidating presence.

Monty answered his question. 'You know what brings us here, young man,' he said in a stern voice. 'Or don't you know that your father is dead?'

'My father ... dead!' The look on the face of the boy was of dismay and disbelief. But Inspector Monty was not one to be fooled. He played his ace card.

'Your mother has told us everything,' he said.

Raj broke down completely. 'I am the culprit,' he said. 'That is why I ran away. It is not her fault. Please don't believe anything my mother says. She will do anything to protect me. I killed my father.'

Monty and Maya now listened to his version of the story. On that fateful night, he had gone to the kitchen to fetch some orange juice for himself. He had been unable to sleep, having had an altercation with his father the same evening.

'What was that about?' Maya asked. Raj looked up, a sad look in his soft, brown eyes. These were not killer eyes, Monty decided.

'You see,' Raj said, 'I live with my friend Ravi here. I had gone to visit my parents for a few days to reveal this to them; I had become sick of hiding my love. So, on the very first day of my arrival there, I got this rock off my chest and told my parents about it. They were shocked.'

He looked down again. 'My mother came to terms with it. My father, however, made my life hell from that day on. He said I was not a man. We argued everyday. Things came to a head on the evening of the day the murder happened. In fact, I had planned to depart that very night. And I was forced to do so, in any case.' His tears fell in gentle plops on his pale, pampered hands.

Ravi put a protective arm around his shoulder and asked him if he wished to stop talking.

'No, let me continue,' said Raj. 'I was surprised to see the kitchen light on. I stepped into the kitchen and saw my father trying to force his attentions onto Sunita. Sunita is like a sister to me. We have grown up together. I was aghast. I ran to fetch the revolver, which I knew was kept in the side cupboard drawer, and returning, shot my father. I just wanted to stop him from doing what he was doing. I did not think that I would kill him.'

Monty did not believe Raj's story. It could be that his fingerprints were on the revolver. However, who did the other two sets belong to? After all, there were three sets of fingerprints on the revolver.

Though Raj had owned up to the murder, they were not convinced. They left after giving Raj a stern warning to stay where he was. If what he said proved to be true, they would return to take him away.

Raj walked up to Maya and said, 'Please, I am the culprit. Please, leave my mother alone.'

'We have to carry on investigations and reach our conclusions,' Monty said. They did not mention to him that they already had someone else owning up to the murder – none other than the maid, Vandana.

As they walked to the car, Monty looked at Maya and said, 'Why does he keep bringing his mother up? Does he think that his mother is the murderer?'

He said again, 'Why were there three sets of fingerprints on the revolver? If two sets belong to Raj and Vandana, whose was the third hand? It could not be Sunita, *na*? What about

Mrs Verma? Or was there someone else also there, of whom we do not know? Also, had three people together tried to kill Colonel Verma?'

Maya nodded. 'There are many questions to be answered.'

* * *

Returning to Delhi, Monty and Maya checked with their department for further developments. They had told the police department to match Mrs Verma's fingerprints with those of the main set of fingerprints on the revolver, the set that had yet to be identified. The report was still to come and they would have to wait.

Monty and Maya decided to meet over dinner at their favourite restaurant, The Broken Bread, so named because when people break bread together, they share a bond of conviviality and friendship with each other. Here, over food and a glass of wine, they discussed the case.

'This case has too many fingerprints,' Maya told Monty. Monty loved the way Maya's eyes danced as she discussed the case with him. He wanted to take her in his arms, but knew that she never mixed business with pleasure. He sighed.

The next morning, they met at Colonel Verma's house. The house had a forlorn air. Sunita led them in. Mrs Verma was waiting for them in the living room. She looked composed and in control of herself. Her crème, printed silk sari offset her fine features well. She had a set of pearls at her throat, and her diamond earrings caught the light as she nodded her head to acknowledge their presence. They sat facing her.

'Good morning, Mrs Verma,' said Monty. 'We are sorry to disturb you, but we have to perform our duty.'

'I quite understand, Inspector,' she answered graciously.

'We wish to know what actually happened that night.'

'Vandana the maid has already owned up to the murder. She has also told you how it happened. What else is there for me to say?'

'We met Raj yesterday, Mrs Verma. You did not tell us that he was here that night. He has owned up to the murder, too. He says that he is responsible for the death of his father.'

A cry of anguish escaped the old lady's lips. 'Raj, my son!' She wailed. 'Oh, why did you do this?'

'He did it to protect you, madam,' said Monty.

'I can take care of myself. He should know that. Oh why did he do this?' She was beside herself.

'Madam, did you commit the crime, or did he, or did the maid? Why don't you tell us the truth?'

'My son is innocent,' Mrs Verma said. 'This is the truth,' she said.

On that fateful night, Sunita had gone to fetch water for herself. Seeing Colonel Verma arrive, she had moved to the side, but he had caught hold of her and tried to embrace her. When she resisted, he had pinned her against the wall. This is what Raj saw as he came down to fetch some orange juice for himself. Aghast, he ran to his mother's room to tell her. This father of his, the so-called paragon of manliness, was a disgrace.

Mrs Verma ran out with Raj. What she saw filled her with disgust. The poor girl was struggling silently, hoping that the Colonel would let go of her. Mrs Verma was blinded with rage.

She ran out and fetched the revolver. Meanwhile, Vandana had also come upon the scene.

Seeing what was on Mrs Verma's mind, Raj and Vandana had tried to take the revolver from her hands. She had resisted them, and fired anyways. The bullet had found its mark.

This was the explanation given by Mrs Verma. She now claimed to be the murderer.

* * *

Any of the three could have killed Colonel Verma: Mrs Verma, her son Raj, or Vandana. All three had a good enough reason. However, if it was Vandana, Raj would not have owned up to the crime. It was the mother or the son. The son seemed incapable of committing the crime. If he had really committed the murder, he would not have run away and left his mother to deal with it. Mrs Verma seemed the likely culprit. But she could be taking the blame now to protect her son. There were more explanations needed. Who was protecting whom? And why had Vandana agreed to take the blame?

The strident ringing of Inspector Monty's mobile cut through the tension in the air like scissors ripping cloth. He reached into his pocket and moved out of the living room, into the hallway. The call was from the police department. The forensic report was in. The third, unidentified set of fingerprints belonged to Mrs Verma. This was the main set of fingerprints around the butt of the revolver. Monty's moustache twitched twice. When it twitched twice, he knew he was on the right track. He could smell his prey now.

Monty went in. He was more or less sure who had

committed the crime. He wanted some further information.

He sat next to Mrs Verma. 'If you committed the crime, as you now claim, why did Vandana agree to take the blame?' he asked her. 'She could not be so devoted a servant as to agree to such a heinous act.'

'I told Vandana that I would look after her daughter, Sunita. I would make sure she had a good marriage and provide for her dowry. You know that such a task is impossible for these poor people. She agreed. She was living for her daughter's sake; her husband had deserted her long ago. She saw the value in my reasoning. It is as simple as that, Inspector.'

She continued talking, 'My son went away at my insistence. I did not want any undue publicity to befall him. It would not be good for the family to have its secrets out in public. Moreover, he did not do anything. He cannot hurt a fly.' Her face softened for a moment, then became tense again.

'I am responsible for everything that goes on in my home. The murder is also my responsibility.' There was a steely edge to her voice now. She was a woman who usually got her way.

She did not get her way this time, though, thought Inspector Monty wryly as he moved forward to take Mrs Verma into custody. He was sure of his prey now. By putting the blame on Vandana, she had thought that she could continue to be there for her son and protect the family name.

Mrs Verma did not weep, and Monty was surprised that he had not noticed her tenacity earlier, thinking of her as a timid, old woman.

'I am glad Raj is with Ravi, Inspector,' she said. 'He will look after Raj in my absence. My son is a good human being. My husband has proved how much of a *man* he was. I have no regrets about killing him.'

Monty and Maya left with Mrs Verma in custody. The dynamic duo of Monty and Maya had solved another case. They would be celebrating with ice cream after lunch, Monty promised himself. As they drove off, he looked at Maya in the rear-view mirror and winked.

Abha Iyengar is a poet, author, essayist and British Council-certified creative writing facilitator. Her writings have been featured in Asian Cha, New Asian Writing, The Asian Writer, Bewildering Stories, Danse Macabre, among others. Her story 'The High Stool' was nominated for the Story South Million Writers Award. She won a Special Jury Prize in Patras, Greece for her poem-film Parwaaz (Flight). She was the Lavanya Sankaran Writing Fellow 2009–2010. Her published works include Yearnings (poetry), Flash Bites (flash fiction) and Shrayan (fantasy).

For more information about the author and her work, visit www.abhaiyengar.com and www.abhaencounter.blogspot.in.

Vietnam

THE HANOI SWORD SWINDLE

WILLIAM L. GIBSON

The last time I was in Southeast Asia, I suddenly found myself without a dime to my name.

I planned to make my way to Kuala Lumpur, to the only person in the region I thought would do me a favour. As the bus rolled along the highway through the seemingly infinite serried lines of the palm plantations, I counted at least three dead monitor lizards, their prehistoric bodies mangled and pulped in the road from the weight of the massive trucks carrying the palm fruit to the processing plants that manufacture the oil that cooks the food of more than a third of the world's population.

I remember seeing a dead monkey in the road, a large male with his skull split and the brain matter, chunky and bright red, spilling onto the asphalt. His little body was prostrate, spread-eagled face down, like the corpse of a wizened old man.

I was heading through this landscape of repetition and road kill to see a woman I knew as Koko Goh, whose beauty was as famous as the ferocity of her temper. Older now, she had settled down in her native land after knocking about Asia for the better part of her life – first as a Triad gangster's moll, then as the head of that unfortunate man's network. (They never did find the rest of his corpse.) Along the way, she had assumed a legendary status as the underworld equivalent of Pol Pot.

There was one story that a two-bit Sino-Laotian hood who ran *ya-baa* for her network once called her a thief, questioned her leadership, and disobeyed an order. He even went so far as to tell her messenger he thought she was 'nothing but a silly cunt.' When Kokie heard this insult, she told the messenger to find out more about the boy's family.

The father was a hard-working merchant who sold tires and gasoline in bottles from a roadside stall near Pakxe. Every morning on the way to work, the father indulged in his one luxury in life: a steamed pork bun. Seven months after he first insulted her, Kokie had the son brought to her, strung up by his feet, trussed like a pig.

After rubbing her vagina in his face while calling him names, she personally castrated him then stuffed his severed penis into his mouth. While he was choking on it, she slit his throat, blood pouring down his face while his legs jerked, his body spinning. She then had his body ground up, seasoned, frozen, and sent to Pakxe. There, he fed his father in meat buns for the next three months.

I heard this horrible story from Kokie herself while gripping the tablecloth in total fear, my knuckles white, trying to laugh along with her. She told me her only regret was that she didn't have the foresight to have the father killed as well after he had eaten the last morsels of his son.

By the time I knew her, Kokie was already so ensconced in power that she had turned to booze and drugs to while away the lonely hours after dark. Eventually 'after dark' became all day, and slowly her empire slipped away while she tripped the light fantastic. Now she ran a tidy little operation in KL, with a brothel upstairs and a small but loyal corps of troops plus a large network of favours and information that would keep her safe for years to come – though even she knew it was only a shadow of her former power.

How she would react to seeing me after all this time and after what I had done to her was an open question. But I remember thinking that I had little choice. What else was I to do – try to live as a pickpocket? Scam European backpackers out of a few dollars? I trusted that Kokie was smart enough to know that my abilities were as strong as ever and that my desperation would prove the most valuable asset she could have. Assuming, of course, that she needed me for something.

I remember thinking that KL was brighter than the last time I had been there. Either the public lighting had improved or my memory was dim. Kokie's place was on a nondescript side street near the Indian Muslim quarter. By day, the windowless building appeared abandoned on a street bustling with pedestrians and noisy with the incessant honking of motor scooters.

By night, only the appearance of a small contingent of Chinese-Malay tough guys lingering by the door flanked by mastiff-sized statues of Chinese lions indicated that the building was inhabited.

The spike-haired toughs stopped chatting in Hokkien and looked me up and down when it became apparent that I was approaching them. Lost tourist? Easy target? As I got closer, I noticed mean-looking, moustachioed Irene leaning behind the lion by the door, just as she had done years before. Her head was shaved now, but the impassive cruelty in the eyes remained the same. She recognized me too, and looked surprised to see me after all this time. Her glare was a cross between incredulousness and apprehension: white ghosts are supposed to remain dead.

'Hi, Irene. Is Koko here?' I asked quietly without staring in her eyes.

With the slightest nod, she pressed a button next to the door, then wordlessly motioned me up the dim stairs that appeared beyond.

Each step creaked as I quickly scaled the two stories to the mauve padded door of Kokie's office. I didn't dare linger too long, for I had learned that bad things have a tendency to dwell in the dark recesses of these old stairways.

Except for one cone of light from a dangling bulb, it was dark as midnight up in her office. She was sitting lotus on cushions beneath the bulb, slightly bowed, next to a low glass-topped desk on which sat an overfilled ashtray and empty glassine bags.

When I went in, she was still as a doll and wrapped in long dark robes, with pitch-black hair hung silken straight across her face and down to the small of her back. In the murky light, she resembled a chrysalis.

At first I thought she was asleep, with her head lolled

forward. She seemed smaller than I remembered and looked a bit rough round the edges from the smokes and the stuff she liked to stick up her nose. Yet even in that degraded state, she still carried a regal charm that belied her having been born in a *kampong* and raised in a brothel on the Thai border, a working girl at twelve. I recall now her lidded bedroom eyes that could tie a man in knots at twenty paces: the colour of gunship iron, yet limpid and moist.

After I had stood for at least thirty seconds before her still form, she lifted those eyes toward me but betrayed no surprise as she said, 'Wah! As I live and breathe! Are you here?'

In my memory, her body is ball-jointed, like one of Bellmer's horrible dolls. She shifted on her little throne of cushions, her body possessed by slow movements and a primal yet balletic elegance, like a butterfly first struggling from its cocoon.

I could tell she was high as a kite, though her sloe-eyes maintained a pellucid quality, as though they had their own internal light source.

'How you doing, Koko?'

A hand with an unlit cigarette appeared from the robes followed by another with a lit match. Her pale white fingers appeared strangely elongated, insect-like. She took a drag, then said, 'Let me think, sailor ... yes, I haven't seen you since you came around here peddling an antique statue of Shiva. It was a fake, no?'

'It was an original thirteenth-century Chola bronze of a *nautch* girl, and it was superb.'

She snorted out a blast of blue cigarette smoke. 'How did that go for you?'

'Enough to get me back to Chicago.'

'Good for you. And you're here now because why?'

'Mistakes were made.'

She snorted at that remark too, then stared straight into my eyes. 'You look good. Still trim. Still fit. Staying strong?' I started to respond, but she continued, 'You stink. What do you want? Did you come here to tell me how beautiful I am?'

I remember saying something I had once before whispered into her ear: 'Your lithe body is an iridescent scabbard of death.'

'Don't make an ass of yourself. There's the door, sailor. Walk out of it before I have you carried out.'

'Come on, Kokie – we're old friends from way back, ain't we? Why do you want to talk to me like that?'

'People like you don't have any friends.'

'Kokie, why be cruel?'

She looked away, stared down at her nails buffed translucent white like opals, shining brightly against the darker hue of the robes. She stayed like that for a full minute, then without looking at me, she said, 'You owe me a lot, and it's not just the money.'

'I know, Koko, and you know I'm good for it. That stuff from the last time, that was a mistake, a misunderstanding. Just business, you understand. You would have done the same thing in my position.'

Still staring at her fingertips, she said thoughtfully, 'I should have you shot.'

'Kokie, it's bad right now, really bad. I've got nothing. I'm totally broke.'

'Maybe you can wash dishes at a noodle stall.'

'We're old pals. We had a good thing there for a while, so

let's keep past things in the past and let sleeping dogs lie.'

She snorted again, staring at her opal nails. 'What are you doing back in Asia anyway, ha?'

I must have sighed. 'It's a long story.'

'You used to like to tell me long stories.'

'You don't want to hear this one.'

She lit another cigarette, watched the smoke pouring off the end before saying, 'I will cut you a deal, sailor.'

She leaned toward me, one small tit peeking out of the folds of her top robe, the nipple thick like a pencil eraser, the small breast showing sag lines.

'You do something for me and I'll not only forgive you for leaving me like you did, but I'll buy you a ticket back to wherever you want. And then, after that, you never come back here, ha? And if you say no, I am sending you out of here with no legs and you never come back here anyway. Either way, if I see you again after you do as I ask, I will have my cousin feed you to his pigs. What do you say to that, sailor?'

In my memory, her limpid eyes are stirringly beautiful, if only because they veiled the coldness of her soul.

'I'm at your service. What do you want me to do?'

She leaned forward. 'You go to Hanoi. There is a man there who owns an antique sword. Some say maybe it belonged to Le Thai To himself, that it is the very sword he used to drive the Chinese from Vietnam. I want it. I will help you get the sword. I want you to verify that it is authentic, then you bring it back to me. Maybe I will want to sell it and you will help me. Then, you go away forever. Simple, ha?'

'Yeah, simple.' I paused to exhale before continuing: 'I thought Thai To gave the sword back to heaven. Who do you think has it now?'

Her face cracked into a devil's smile I'd only seen once before. Her lips curled back across her teeth, yellow like lacquered bamboo, nostrils flared. It was not a good sign. She remained smiling as she spoke, 'The sword is owned by the son of the Chairman of the Council of State of the Communist Party of Vietnam.'

'Oh, that's good. That simplifies everything. You want me to fly to Hanoi, ask this nice man if I can borrow his antique sword for an hour, then fly back here with it, is that it?'

Her brimstone smile remained in place. 'My cousin's pigs are very hungry. He does not care well for them at all.'

I had no choice, but I didn't come to Koko looking for choices. I had wanted a means of escape, and perhaps indirectly she was offering me one.

'OK, but you've got to give me more information. Plus, I'll need a new passport, with plenty of stamps in it – it can't look like I just came straight from America – and I need a visa.'

'All in due time, sailor, all in due time. You told me before you were a magician, remember? Then you disappeared with my money. So now you make some new magic. Get me my sword. And, if you think about going to Hanoi and disappearing again, you are not thinking right.'

She lifted a small bell from the folds of her robe and rang it softly, once. The door opened noiselessly to reveal a compact person with a bristle cut. I wasn't sure at first if it was a man or a woman.

'This is Tan Siew Kok.'

She was one of those amazingly fit, miniscule Asian women with matchstick-thin legs and wrists. Her taut body was like a bundle of paper clip wire covered with dark parchment. Her hair was cut short, gelled into short spikes. A small stud fitted into one nostril and her rook-black eyes glared at me as if I were maggot-infested meat. The face, however, remained perfectly slack.

'Does she speak English?'

'No. And make no mistake, she isn't here to help you, ha? She's here to watch you for me.' Then, in Mandarin, 'Siew Kok, show him.'

From beneath her black silk blouse, the fierce woman produced a thin silver chain with a small, shrivelled thing the size of a cocktail cornichon dangling from it.

'Is that what I think it is?' I remember saying, then leisurely bending down to inspect it, 'Hmm. He must have been Chinese.'

She barked at Kokie in Chinese, 'Let me kill him now, please! I want his *ang moh* cock on a string!'

I remember thinking of an oblique retort but stopped cold when I felt the blade against my larynx. I hadn't even seen her hand move. I was bent over like an arthritic septuagenarian, that dead Chinaman's prick in my fingers.

I heard Kokie shout 'No!', and the knife vanished as quietly as it appeared. This time, I at least noticed her arm moving. I never did see the blade.

Straightening, a rivulet of sweat running down my cheek, I turned as casually as I could to face Kokie while I spoke, 'So to accept your offer, let me be clear. You want me to go to Hanoi to get this antique sword and sweetie here is supposed to watch over me – make sure I come back, is that it?' She nodded. 'And what if I don't come back?'

'You will.'

Feeling assured, I asked 'And what if I don't come back with China Dyke in one piece?'

She snorted again. 'Then you answer to her sister!' She laughed a short, sharp high note that resembled a peregrine's shriek.

'So what's it going to be, sailor? You bring me the sword, I set you free. Or I have Siew Kok kill you and she can parade around KL with your dried prick on a chain?'

'You leave me no choice.'

'You made your choice. Maybe you should have stayed in Chicago, ha? So what's it going to be? Deal?'

'How much time do I have?'

A relaxed smile on her face, she exhaled a mushroom of smoke. 'You have one month.' She then lowered her head and resumed the same creepy calm pose as when I arrived.

As I turned to go, she said aloud to no one, 'I have all the time in the world.'

*　*　*

Koko chartered a flight into Hanoi. I was posing as a travelling businessman who insured shipments of perishable goods. Siew Kok was my regional guide from Malaysia. Neither of us spoke Vietnamese, but we were to rendezvous with an associate of Kokie's in the capital.

My one consolation on the flight was that if Kokie wanted me dead, then I reckoned I would have already been pig shit, my shrivelled cock hanging from her caitiff's neck. Otherwise, the prospect was so bad as to be absurd.

I remember also feeling something I would come to recognize with more frequency: the metaphysical pangs of aging. At this point, I hadn't been a young man for quite some time, but until that plane ride, with that freak-show Chinese lesbian sitting ramrod straight in the seat next to me, I suddenly felt incredibly tired and weak.

Plus, I had been stupid to go to Kokie. It was a mistake I wouldn't have made fifteen years earlier, but would have made twenty-five years before: it was an amateur mistake. Was I getting slack?

It was a horrible recognition, but for the first time, I wanted off the ride. To take a leap from the merry-go-round. Deal me out, I've had enough of this bullshit.

I must have uttered a tired man's sigh, because China Dyke glared at me with more contempt than ever.

I leaned over to push the moment, 'So, sweetie, ever been to Hanoi before? Lovely place.'

She purred in Mandarin without twitching a muscle of her face, 'When we are finished, I will be allowed to tear your tongue from your mouth and shove it up your ass before stuffing your ugly smelly cock in its place so you will always speak with cock breath, you filthy goat bastard.'

'Hmm, too bad. It really is nice this time of year. Northern Vietnamese girls are perfectly charming. The first thing they ask is, "Where are you from?", then "Do you like Vietnam?", then "Would you like a Vietnamese wife?" Perfectly charming.'

'Koko told me she wants to watch while I slice open your scrotum. She wants to roll your balls like marbles in her hands before tossing them to the pigs. Personally, I'd rather stick them in the empty bleeding eye sockets of your severed head.'

'I couldn't agree more. It was a stupid war and the Vietnamese suffered far worse than the Americans can know, perhaps can even understand. But look at it now! If Uncle Ho weren't a wax dummy under glass, he'd be turning in his grave!'

'You won't talk so much once I've pulled your teeth from your skull and fed them to you.'

'I wonder if they still serve dog meat? The last time I was there you could get it, but only in a certain section of town. It's not good meat. It's greasy and tough, as you'd expect. But, of course, this was decades ago.'

'Killing you will be one of the highest joys of my life. I have a special place in my trophy cabinet all ready for your disgusting sausage, which I will preserve with great care.'

'I think despite everything, you and I will have a wonderful trip together,' I said and patted her knee. She grabbed my wrist then smiled at me, showing tiny, razor-sharp teeth like a piranha.

I smiled back.

For years, I've prided myself on my pitch-perfect Mandarin, which I learned intimately from the daughter of a Beijing diplomat in Budapest. And Kokie knew I spoke the language of the Celestial Kingdom. She should have warned her minion. That was Kokie's mistake.

Maybe I wasn't so old after all.

* * *

Frankly, I was curious to see Hanoi. I hadn't been there for years and the drawn-out process of *doi moi* was still only at a midway point during that visit. Gone were the legions on bicycles; when I was there, everyone had a dirty putt-putting 155cc scooter, the tiny streets jammed with the damn things, an entire city continuously jostling at 15 km per hour. But everyone had seemed generally happy. For the first time in generations, there was money and calories enough to go around. And a younger generation fed on satellite television and the Internet had begun to shrug off the old ways.

Yet Hanoi had not, at least on my previous visit, fully joined the great Western pornotopia of instantaneous *petit bourgeois* satisfactions, the endless orgy of fat and salt and sugar and the incessant promises of perpetual orgasm.

There was the golf course they were building near the airport and a few low-rise hotels, but generally, other than the increased noise and pollution of the scooter traffic, the city seemed prosperous and happy. So now, after decades of World Trade Organization standards, I was curious to know if the place had gone full-tilt into the whirlpool of Western progress.

As the plane banked over the city, I remember seeing Ho Hoan Kiem, the Lake of the Restored Sword, the Tortoise Stupa on its own islet sliding quickly from view as the plane banked again toward the airport. The stupa was intact, as it would be, a symbol of the city like the Eiffel Tower in Paris or the Empire State Building in New York, but it was dwarfed now by the glass-skin skyscrapers of the upmarket business and residential complexes ringing the lake.

It was into this lake in the Fifteenth Century that Le Thai To was supposed to have returned the celestial sword to a giant tortoise – the very sword I was now flying into Hanoi to claim. It is said that there are tortoises still living in the lake that are five hundred years old, which would date them to the time of Thai To. There is a rumour that a blade discovered by a fisherman in this very lake bore the inscription 'By The Will of Heaven.' These homespun stories blend historical fact with urban myth and a dose of spirituality.

In point of fact, there are two stories of the sword.

There is the famous one that gave birth to the myth of the lake, the story of the giant golden tortoise that rose from the depths to reclaim the divine sword Thai To used to defeat the Chinese invaders.

The other story, the hidden one, is that the general's sword was passed down from one generation of the ruling elite of North Vietnam to the next: that the sword was wielded like a royal sceptre by the family that could lay claim to the power of Hanoi. Any Vietnamese who held the celestial sword of Le Thai To ruled the country from Hanoi to Hue.

What Koko Goh thought she was going to do with it in Malaysia was no concern of mine.

The taxi ride from the airport disclosed a new Vietnam. Gone, for the most part, were the once ubiquitous motorbikes that clogged the streets. Now there were cars. Congestion was so heavy city officials had to close the thirty-six streets of the Old Quarter to vehicular traffic.

At least this saved the old banyans that crept over the sidewalks, though now the pedestrian zone was antiseptic, clean and brightly painted, managed entirely by a French theme park company. As a result, the new Old Quarter bore as much resemblance to the one of my memories as the old Times Square did to the new. The place was now safe for groups of affluent teenagers to stroll alone at night as they window-shopped and chatted on flashy silver and red phones that bore a hammer-and-sickle logo. Yet not far away, the true city lurked.

By night, behind the brightly painted facades, down rheumy passageways tilting at crazy angles in the irregular, low-wattage lights, the old conurbation throbbed with life.

The French theme park owners felt content to leave the enhancements only skin deep, friable to any who chose to penetrate. The ancient city, the one that stood here before Hanoi was given a name, a city called Thang Long, City of the Rising Dragon, had a spirit that remained in the maple-leaf pattern of the old quarter and still dwelled in the narrow dankness of the creeping banyans.

Yet the Hanoi I saw on that trip was already far gone. The Temple of Literature – whose cornerstone, they say, was laid in the Western year of 1070 – had to be annually sprayed with polyethylene to keep it from crumbling in the noxious clouds of automobile exhaust.

The rusty wing of a B-52 bomber that used to jut from a shallow pond, the jaunty Stars and Stripes of the American Air Force still clearly visible as a monument to the bombing of Hanoi, seemed to be forgotten. When I asked where I could find it, I only got wild stares. Either no one knew what I was talking about or this was something no one talked about anymore.

China Dyke, contrariwise, appeared to be having the time of her life. From taxi windows, her gaze would linger almost as long on the Jimmy Choo shoes as on the elegant salesgirls with delicate ankles behind the glass counters. Yet she rarely left my side and always had one eye on me.

She let me go to the toilet alone, though she hovered outside as a mother does with a son who uses the big-boys bathroom for the first time. Getting her out of my way wouldn't be easy and, worse still, at this point I had no idea how I would do it.

We were to meet our contact at the Mausoleum of Ho Chi Minh, a modest version of Lenin's tomb that the Soviets had built for Ho's eternal enshrinement. On my last visit, it had been thronged with Vietnamese on what amounted to a patriotic *Haj*; this second visit only revealed busloads of bored foreign tourists cruising around the grounds.

In death, Uncle Ho was accorded an ignominious afterlife as a diminutive wax-work in a black suit, his wispy grey beard reattached every few years.

This was a fate he hadn't wanted: his will was to be cremated, his ashes buried in separate spots across the country. Now, instead, the offspring of his vanquished enemies came on bus tours to gawk at the corpse of the skinny man who spoke close to ten languages, used over a hundred aliases, had travelled the world from Brooklyn to Bangkok, and after his death was transfigured as the saviour of the Vietnamese people.

Since we were to maintain our cover, we played at being tourists, and went in to see the man himself. I noted that Ho's honour guard had shrunk from five ramrod-straight soldiers to one stooped figure, slouching in what was surely considered punitive duty.

Outside, China Dyke sat bored beside me while we waited on a bench beside dusty shrubbery for our contact to appear. Smiling tourists milled about, shading their eyes from the intense sun. A few Vietnamese youth strayed about under conical hats, posing for pictures with the foreigners. Some even dressed in camouflage fatigues with hard green pith helmets toting toy Kalashnikovs, living images from American films. There were even a few domestic tourists in cheap rubber flip-flop sandals that separated them from other Asian visitors, who preferred more robust Western-style leather sandals which on small Asian feet seemed faintly absurd, like Roman children playing at being senators.

From this throng, a tall woman in a flowing white *ao dai* caught my attention. She moved with a purposeful dignity that indicated she wasn't a local dressing old-fashioned for snapshots with sunburnt Europeans. Under the bright sun, the *ao dai* that clung to her exiguous body created a hallucinatory effect so that she seemed to shimmer in and out of view, like a mirage.

It was as though she wasn't really there. The woman was a vision from an idealized past, a ghostly Vietnam long since relegated to the dust heap.

In my memory, I see the scene from above, her gliding through the multitude, distinct in her own light, circling ever closer to where we sat, yet miraculously invisible in the crowd.

In reality, she had found a perfect disguise. The locals would automatically dismiss someone so badly out of fashion, while the tourists only saw another exotic species on display.

As she approached, she never so much as brushed shoulders with another person but glided through the mass of sweating humanity, cool as a breeze. I glanced over to China D to find her eyes locked on the advancing woman – so I wasn't the only one who was aware of her.

From her lissom body jutted high, firm breasts with the heft of ripe golden pears, stretching the thin material of the *ao dai*, and a stalk neck that seemed nearly too thin to be human. Wisps of black hair curled behind her ears in the heat, tapering delicately like the fine ends of a paint brush. Her soft jaw-line ended in a small chin that narrowed the broad face into a triangle. Large brown pupils shielded by double-lidded eyes peered beneath the raven-black eyebrows, soft and sparse as butterfly antennae.

'Hello, are you interested in Vietnamese history?' She spoke English with an accent peculiar to Vietnamese, yet I detected another accent underlying this one.

'Hello ... yes, we are. I'm Mr Bencoolen, and this is my assistant, Olan.'

'If you're here on holiday, Mr Bencoolen, Hanoi has many attractions to offer.'

'Indeed, my friend Kokie tells me that there's a famous antique district.'

'Ah, you like antiques?'

'Swords, especially.'

Without a change in demeanour, she said, 'My name is Nguyen Au Co, but Western people call me Pearl.'

'Pearl? How quaint. Shall we go for a walk?'

Her knees suddenly thrust out and she was squatting before us. 'Act like you're asking me directions,' she said.

I pulled a small map from my sweat-stained shirt pocket. 'Kokie explained to you why we're here?'

'Yes,' and again her voice lilted away from Vietnamese, but I couldn't place the undergirding accent.

'Do we have a plan for obtaining the sword, or should we simply ask the nice man if we can take away his pride and joy?'

She smiled at me, pointed at the map, then across the

plaza. 'Yes, a simple plan. Mr Tran has a playboy of a son who likes to frequent a certain bar. It is there that I will make contact with him. Our sources tell us that this son likes to keep the sword in the bedroom of his private apartment as a decoration.'

She stood up again and said loudly, 'Why not refresh yourself in an air-conditioned museum, such as that one over there? It tells the history of our struggle with the French.' Then she whispered, 'Don't stand until I walk away.'

'But how will we get inside of Tran's son's house? The man must have protection like Caesar.'

She smiled at me, then seemed to nod at China D. 'His son has the weakness all men have.'

'And that's where you come into the picture. You're our honey trap, our *toc dai*?'

'*Toc dai*? You know something about Vietnam?'

'I know a *toc dai* when I see one, even one as lovely as yourself.'

She smiled without showing teeth. 'Everyone is good at something, Mr Bencoolen.'

'So I've been told.'

She leaned forward and cocked her head to one side so that her raven black hair cascaded downward to me. 'What are you good at?'

'Recovery.'

'And do you keep what you recover?'

'I don't work for a percentage.'

Her lips curved into a smile as she spoke. 'Enjoy the museum. Quickly tell me the name of your hotel.'

Smile in place, she rose and pivoted on one heel, the *ao dai* flaring to reveal the baggy pants momentarily clinging like wet cellophane to her valentine ass before she glided away. I turned to China D to take her measure, but she was mesmerized beyond words.

Laughing, I said, 'Don't you know anything about women? Don't sit there with your tongue hanging out, panting like an alley dog. That's no way to start a romance.' I patted her on the knee, and she reflexively grasped my wrist without taking her eyes from the receding figure. 'Don't worry your pretty little head. Your time with her will come – it does for us all.'

She painfully twisted my wrist as she snorted in Mandarin, 'Other than inserting your severed penis into your foul mouth before slitting your throat, the greatest joy of my life will be to fuck that Vietnamese goddess. She is heaven on earth.' Then she faced me, gave my immobile wrist one more squeeze, and said, 'Why do you always have the stench of rotten mud? I will call you "buffalo" while I slaughter you.'

As I rubbed my wrist, I smiled at her and remember saying, 'I know, darling, I know.'

* * *

I was enjoying an ice cold Hanoi beer on the terrace of our hotel overlooking the Red River. From this vantage point, I could barely see, just under a small tarpaulin, a man roasting some sort of small animal in a skillet over a fire fuelled with waste paper. I was admiring his dedication when the phone rang.

China D answered from inside the room, spoke quickly in a Chinese dialect I didn't recognize – Hakka? Teochew? – then called to me in some of the few English words she wanted me to know that she knew: 'Buffalo-man, phone call.'

'Hello. This is Pearl. I have some news for you. We're to meet at Mr Tran's son's favourite bar ....'

'What kind of place is it? Playboy's delight?'

'Please don't interrupt me, Mr Bencoolen, that isn't polite.'

'I'm sorry.'

'As I was saying, we are to meet there. You will not recognize me. This is only the first phrase of the operation.'

'Phase.'

'Excuse me?' Her voice perfectly polite, never registering any emotion, no accentuation except this strange inflection undergirding the Vietnamese.

'Phase, not phrase.'

'I'm sorry?'

'You said "phrase" ... well, it doesn't matter.'

'I don't understand.'

'Listen, where are you from?' A pause. I wasn't playing by the rules.

'I'm sorry Mr Bencoolen, I was explaining our meeting.'

'You're not Vietnamese, are you?'

Another pause. 'I am.'

'Did you study abroad? Switzerland? Germany?'

'Mr Bencoolen, we'll meet at a bar called Cocktail Larry and you will not recognize me.'

'Seoul? Did you spend time in Korea?'

'No, Mr Bencoolen, I've never been to Korea.'

'I have. It's a beautiful country. I remember it snowing in the spring during a freak storm. Have you ever seen snow?'

'Mr Bencoolen ...' Her impatience was expressed not with

a change in tone but in a rushing of syllables, then, finally, surrender: 'I am from Cholon.'

Of course! Cholon, the Chinatown of Saigon, an East within an East. She was Sino-Viet. I should have guessed. Kokie only ever trusted other Chinese, and she only ever trusted people who owed her, in the Vietnamese conception, *nghīa*: devoted love, complete, of mind, body, and spirit.

'Do you get home to Saigon often?'

'No, Mr Bencoolen. Ho Chi Minh City. It hasn't been Saigon in a long time.'

'It will always be Saigon.'

She laughed at that, a wonderfully light, chromatic laugh, dainty but filled with a warm colour that betokened strong blood. 'Yes, yes, that's right. It will always be Saigon,' and then she paused her laughter, checking her unprofessional behaviour.

I followed her lead. 'So, we meet you at Cocktail Barry?'

'Cocktail Larry.'

'Right; I meant Cocktail Larry. Pretend to not recognize you, then what?'

'Then you wait.'

'At the bar?'

'Anywhere you like.'

'I don't understand.'

'Mr Tran's son keeps the sword at home, on display.'

'And so we wait for you at the bar ...?'

'So that Koko knows that I go with Mr Tran's son.'

Witness the act as closely as possible. I remember realizing that other than waiting to assassinate me once my role was complete, this was China D's other job. She couldn't go with

Pearl into the dragon's lair, but she could stand sentry.

'What happens when you're … once you have the sword?'

'I return to Cocktail Larry.'

'Then?'

'Then we go.'

'With the sword?'

She laughed again her clean, ascending, chromatic laugh. 'No. We all go separately. Then we meet at your hotel and I will hand the sword to you. Understand now? OK? Good-bye.'

'Good-bye.'

She clicked off. The plastic of the phone was hot in my hand.

My beer had gone warm too, though I needed the time to think, so I swished it down. China D had switched on the television, tuned in an Argentine soap opera dubbed into Vietnamese. Watching her watching TV with one eye on the screen and one eye on me, I reasoned I would need money if I were to get away from this exterminator of Kokie's. I picked up the phone again, dialled Kokie in KL.

'I've tried to explain to Siew Kok that we need more money. Pearl seems to think we're going to be here for several weeks, perhaps even a month, more.'

'And so, sailor, you have a place to be? You wait until you finish the job.'

'But we need cash. We're not going to get that sword out of here without bribes, never mind the cost of living. Like I said, I tried to explain, but Siew Kok's English isn't very good.'

'Neither is your Chinese,' and in the split-second after she said that I could intuit that it flashed into Kokie's mind that she hadn't warned China D that I could understand their secret language. Impossible to say exactly what it was, the aspiration of the last word suddenly strangled, perhaps. Kokie didn't let her card drop, of course, but I could still read her hand, and I was sure that from here on China D would refrain from her Mandarin outbursts.

No matter; I knew at least what they had in store for me, though Siew Kok's Chinese tendency to the supercilious when dealing with barbarians like myself, her habit of unintentionally spilling the beans, would have proven useful.

'So it's agreed, we get more cash?'

A longish pause as she mulled it over, the sound of a cigarette being sucked on, smoke exhaled, then 'How much?'

'At least fifty-thousand American.'

'What? Ha? You think I send you that much, ha?'

'Kokie, we need to bribe our way through customs, most likely both here and in Malaysia. It won't be cheap. Plus, I think we should move around more in Hanoi – each time we see Pearl, we should get a new hotel under different names. Then there's the extra security precautions, which won't be cheap, either.'

'Ha! Ha!' Twice harshly; that could be good or bad. 'You move around, you attract attention, so you stay put. Ha! Ha! Ha!' From the three 'ha's' I knew I was getting to her. The sound of another drag on the cigarette, then she said, 'OK, OK, OK. So, cash wired to you?'

'No wires; we need a courier.'

'Courier? Courier? Ha! Ha!'

'Kokie?'

'Courier so much more money. Special arrangements. More outlay for me!' She was getting worked up.

'If you wire it, they can track the funds. We need cold hard cash. Can we do this?' I could hear tapping on the other end of the line. 'Kokie, you wanted me to help you with this operation. How badly do you want that sword?'

A long pause followed by an outburst: 'OK, OK, OK ... ha, courier.' Then she swore so quickly in Hokkien, Cantonese, Khmer, Malay, and Thai that I could barely understand that she was complaining simultaneously in five languages that my whore mother's cunt smelled like rancid goat's butter.

Then suddenly, she said, 'Now I need to speak with Siew Kok.'

Once on the phone, China D turned her back to me and began speaking with a belt-drive tongue, switching between Chinese dialects and not using Mandarin. It was clear I would no longer be able to slip inside their code system. Nonetheless, within a few days, a courier arrived with a bag full of cash.

* * *

Three weeks later, we executed our plan. Cocktail Larry's was the kind of swank joint that, like wine bars and golf courses, had become the hallmark of new money the world over. Slim and pretty yet expressionless waitresses served expensive whiskey in heavy crystal tumblers on dark oak tables with thick glass ashtrays. A live piano player tinkled what was meant to pass for jazz but sounded more like a child playing scales. The decor attempted to invoke an imagined Golden Age of American plenty, of steakhouses and martinis, Dean Martin and Frank Sinatra.

The place felt like a movie set. It was a simulacrum of

simulacrums designed to accord with a decadence in which politicos could lounge in loafers while their high-heeled doxies delicately sipped iced gin and their gangster bodyguards fingered their compact automatic pistols. The real blood and dirt in the streets was kept as far from sight as possible.

China D ordered straight whiskey, which she slugged back while striking a pose of cool menace. I watched her make brief eye contact with the fetching young escort of a portly man in a dark three-piece suit. The two smiled at each other with a silent juvenile thrill at living out the life on the silver screen in their own heads. It's a doomed civilization in which even the thugs can't separate reality from deception.

I sipped my imported beer slowly.

The place was noisy, the piano barely audible above the din of conversation. I heard American English and craned my neck to see a titanic man, red-faced, with a beefy paw around a stunning girl who was giggling and sucking at the ice in her glass. Not far away, the image was repeated in the person of a Russian, and then again, as in a fun-house mirror, the image reappeared, only this time with ... a Korean, perhaps. The Vietnamese mostly kept to their own tables, the girls swishing in brand-name dresses. There were no tourists in this joint.

The bar suddenly went dead quiet except for the sound of the piano player, whose finger stuck on a note too long with his foot on the sustain pedal. For a brief moment, the only sound was a high C#, which faded away before the din picked up again and the piano player resumed his tune. In the reflection of a mirror, I, too, had seen Pearl enter the bar. In that same mirror, I watched China D's eyes widen as her mouth slacked into a soundless oval.

Pearl was wearing a thigh-length Chinese cheongsam with stiletto heels, and nothing else. At first, I thought that the black dress was printed with glittering black flowers, but it was not reflected light. The patterns were formed from pin-hole perforations, and those dazzling tiny white dots were glimpses of her flesh intensified by the darkness of the dress, a liquid skin that had slit to the thighs enough to reveal the first curve of the smooth globe of her ass.

Every aspect of her body flowed in controlled circles except her neck and head, which she kept immobilized, as though the Mandarin collar of the dress locked her posture erect. She held her head above the crowd, calm and still with a farouche smile that she cast at no one. As she glided through the room sidestepping obstacles as though they were made of air, there wasn't a male mouth that didn't quiver, nor a female eye that didn't sharpen with envy.

'That's our girl,' I sighed. China D didn't pay any attention to me. Her sight was blinded to all, save this idol floating in our midst.

Pearl finally came to rest at the bar, one leg slightly forward, the knee provocatively raised, as though waiting to be touched. She ordered an iced tea, sipping through the straw with a daintiness that let her take in the room while creating an intimation of availability, though at a price beyond most of the mere mortals arrayed before her.

It wasn't long before our target, a short, unattractive man in his twenties with a body sculpted and moulded by daily hours spent in a gym approached without caution and slotted next to her. It wasn't two minutes before his palm had dropped to the proffered knee, though the flirtations and negotiations continued for more than an hour.

I watched fascinated as Pearl worked her charms. She could simply have said 'yes' to the advances, but that would have led to a hotel and a quick bang. Her manoeuvre was to get into the man's home, alone and away from his praetorian guard, and then abscond with the sword by whatever means necessary. I imagine this could have involved perhaps even killing the boy, but what business was that of mine?

From across the room, we watched them engage in the ancient ritual of sexual commerce. Their coded body language was easy enough to read. At first, she is taken aback by his forwardness. He moves in closer. She backs away again incredulously while letting his hand move further up her thigh. Their departure together was only a matter of time.

China D sat steaming beside me, throwing back whiskey after whiskey, her sense of duty blunted first by jealous rage, then increasingly by the alcohol sloshing around her stomach. When the man slipped a strong arm around Pearl's waist and propelled her toward the door, China D clenched her fist so tightly that she nearly cracked the crystal in her hand. She remained white-knuckled while we waited for Pearl's return. I guessed that her whiskey-addled imagination was animating all sorts of sexual derring-do between Pearl and our mark.

I knew better. Four, five … seven thrusts, and it would be over. The boy would roll off and our Pearl would be no more distressed than if she'd dropped a hankie.

I kept an eye on both the clock and China D's whiskey intake. How much could she consume? When Pearl returned to the bar a little less than ninety minutes later, her exterior was as smooth as silk. Whatever had transpired back in Tran's son's home, I was never to know. She nodded at us then and turned her attention back to the bar. Mission accomplished, and time for us to go.

China D stood and, to my surprise, maintained her deadly balance as we walked, but the whiskey had obviously taken its toll. When I tried to catch her as she slipped on the cracked pavement, she spat a curse in Hokkien, then querulously slapped me away. She was loaded to the gills and dangerous from witnessing such sacrilege. Tonight, all men were to be eliminated, casually yet painfully. Her goddess waited only a few miles away in a hotel room, and I doubt it was planned that I would leave that hotel all of one body.

But unlike my warden, I had been to Hanoi before.

The locals brew up a potent rice-based vodka they call *zeo*. Truly filthy stuff; in the olden days they simply fermented rice in a large clay pot, mixing in flavouring, ginseng, mushrooms, spices. Several months later, the resulting gunk was pressed to extract the juice. It was a simple home brew that created a drunk akin to a narcotic high.

I'd had it before, during my last visit. After finishing one bottle, the horizon fell off toward the left, lights tracing downward as one's thoughts lofted away from the importunate scintilla of the five senses into an enchanted realm of dragons and courtesans while the body itself nodded and dragged like that of a junkie on high. They sold this shit from stalls on the street.

We were moving through the old part of the city on foot, down an alleyway slick with something putrid, away from the shopping zone the French had established. I remember vividly the banyans hanging low over us in the heat, scattering the light from the overhead street lamps. Faces would suddenly loom up from the gloom, some laughing, drunken, some sullen.

Half-hidden in this murky phantasmagoria, an old woman without teeth was selling *zeo* from a small table stall. It was the homemade goodie, poured into mismatched bottles, just like I remembered.

Without haggling, I bought three bottles and handed one to China D, who contemptuously sneered at me while taking a big swill. Her pride wouldn't allow her to show her disgust, and after I took a big gulp of my own, she grinned while taking down another for herself. I nearly retched on my next gulp. The stuff could take the sheen off marble. After we had finished one bottle, she hailed a passing motor-cyclo.

Despite her paling complexion, we shared the second bottle as we rode. I was already beginning to reel, my vision spin and drift, but without a bellyful of scotch, I at least had a fighting chance against Kokie's killer, who had begun to swat at imaginary insects.

'Fucking night wasps, damned annoying,' she muttered in Mandarin, her head lolling.

In the hotel room, my chaperone fell over the writing table, sending sheets of paper flying like scattered doves as she pirouetted toward the bed. I managed to crash into the desk chair, my head slumped, the carpet beneath me undulating while the room rolled over silent swells. She lay motionless for a few moments, then raised herself up and staggered toward the bathroom from whence came the sound of heaving and the smell of vomit.

Swaying and weaving like a sailor on shore leave, she emerged to tie my hands and feet to the chair with rough thin cord. I didn't bother to struggle. Even drunk, her jujitsu would flatten me before I got to the door.

'So when is our new girlfriend going to show up?' I wondered aloud. 'She might find this kind of kinky.'

Sitting upright on the bed opposite me, China D's head hung to one side, but still she stayed awake, blade in hand, watching me with a flushed grimace and blood-red eyes. We were bound in a weird nightmare of incoherent yet potentially lethal surveillance of one another. The moonshine tinted the room purple so that this immobile game seemed to be taking place on Pluto. I've no idea how long we waited – time had lost all meaning. The coded knock sounded on the door. Without turning her back to me, China D staggered to answer it. Pearl strode in, transformed into a nondescript girl in loose denim jeans and a cheap baggy sweatshirt on which was printed Uncle Ho's jolly face, a marshmallow-yellow hammer-and-sickle floating behind his head. I stayed quiet in the small chair by the writing desk, kicking loose papers under the bed. Pearl first sat, then reclined on the mattress.

Her hair was now high in a tight knot, her face radiant without make-up and only inches from China D's vicious small hands. Her own hands casually clutched a large woman's bag, from which she slipped a wrapped parcel no larger than a mid-sized aubergine. She placed it on the bedside table, beside the third unopened bottle we'd bought from the old woman.

'Are you drinking *zeo*?,' she asked with mirth in her voice. Pretending not to notice my restraints, she purred, 'Perhaps you would like a drink, Mr Bencoolen?'

The thought made me nauseous, but I nodded my assent. She reached for the bottle, leaning long and thin like a stalk of bamboo bending in the wind, across the prostrate figure of China D. The effect was electrifying, and the little villain on the bed went stiff.

She poured two full measures in the thick glasses on the writing desk, took one in her hand, then sat upright again, to give me a salute before sipping some. My glass remained on the desktop.

'I have the sword handle. There is no blade. It's there, in that parcel. Would you like to see it?'

Neither of us answered.

'Siew Kok? Mr Bencoolen?' She looked amused, took another sip from the glass, and made a sour face. 'I think this *zeo* is too strong for me. Siew Kok, would you like some?' And without waiting for an answer, she leaned back, limber bamboo in the breeze, to place the heavy glass in China D's slim hand, their faces inches apart.

She was thus smoothly elongated when the ninja dyke made her move. In one motion, she leapt forward to lock Pearl in an embrace that could either be a prelude to lust or the python's first squeeze. None of us seemed sure which it would be, but Pearl's lips were on her own and the decision was made. I tried to stand, but the room was spinning from the *zeo* and my restraints seemed to have grown even tighter.

I'm sure in real time it didn't take long, but under the effects of the Vietnamese hooch, the unfolding softness was nearly too much to endure, a softness like a Dali painting with the same lack of perspective in which details magnify then feather away. There were blank spots, as though the film were missing reels, so I wasn't always sure what I was watching unfold on the bed while tied in that chair.

China D was completely naked, while Pearl had her sweatshirt off, Uncle Ho's sunshine face singing to me from the floor. China D's scrawny body was thin like wire, hairless except for the little patch of supremely dark hair above her narrow slit. Against Pearl's moon-white skin, her flesh appeared especially dusky. Her nipples were dark spikes that Pearl's red lips lovingly sucked, her black hair now spilling over China D's thin ribs.

Moving upward, Pearl's own breasts were then pressed against the smaller woman beneath her, their prolonged kissing rough and masculine. China D's little body began to press upward as a man would against a heavier woman or a woman a man above her. Her thin legs spread to enwrap Pearl's waist, right on the edge of the woman's jeans, pushing downward as though the pants would easily roll down those oyster thighs.

Pearl responded with a contrapuntal rhythm, rubbing herself along the smaller woman pinioned beneath her. Did she have China D's wrists above her head, clasped in one strong hand? Where was the blade?

And then the darkness washed over me and when I surfaced, the women were now reversed, with China D atop Pearl, the jeans still in place, while China D rubbed her dark pencil-stub nipples against the larger pink aureoles of Pearl's swelling breasts. My eyes fixed on the osculating circles while the two nipped at one another's necks and collar bones. Pearl's fingers slid down China D's narrow body, then ascended right between the skinny thighs of the smaller woman above her, in a perfect doggy position with her ass pitched in the air. I remember a painful erection.

It seemed we all shared the pleasurable shock when the

smooth fingers entered her. How long does she finger the tiny assassin above her? How tight, how delicious, could the killer's cunt be?

Blackness again. When I came to, the women were flipped again, with Pearl above the other, driving with force four slim fingers into the other, the smaller body rocking in a bliss far greater than she could have anticipated. Orgasm followed orgasm, the small body vibrating and futilely grasping at the pumping arm, flailing to bring the pleasure to a close, failing to end the euphoria her body could barely handle. Pearl's face was serene as a statue throughout this procedure, the fingers of one hand slipped in the smaller woman's vagina, the fingers of the other hand stuffed in the mouth trying to shout.

The entire room heaved, lurched to the left, then went black.

Next I remember Pearl was standing above me with the zipped money bag in her hand. She'd dressed, Uncle Ho on the sweatshirt covering her perfect globes, the nipples denting the cloth. A half-conscious movement of my mouth toward them, and she simply put her hand on my forehead and pushed my head back. I only then realized that my limbs were free.

'Sit still, sailor,' she said in polite tones, though her face was flushed from the recent exertion. China D was naked with her eyes closed, drooling, sound asleep on the bed. In my lap was a small bundle of American money.

'Mr Bencoolen,' she said, still standing above me, 'that packet contains five thousand American dollars.'

I glanced at the table. The parcel was gone. She leaned down into my face, lifted my heavy head by the chin to gaze into my eyes. 'You're not a nice man. I could have you killed so very easily, but, like most of your type, you've blundered into something far larger than you could realize. You are an innocent. You are ...'

I managed to sputter a slurred word, 'simple?'

She smiled at me as she raised her supple frame, 'Yes; simple you are, Mr Bencoolen. And so you live. I give you twenty-four hours to leave Hanoi. And I suggest that you never return to Vietnam.'

She turned to go, but I called out, more forcibly than I thought I could, 'I don't understand. Who do you work for? What's the big deal about this damn sword without a blade?'

She swivelled to face me. 'What Koko intended to do with this weapon is not honourable. It is a disgrace and it violates the *nghĩa* that we share. '*Xót thay chút nghĩa cũ càng, Dau lìa ngó ý còn vuong to long.*' Do you understand? 'With bitter regret, she recalled her first love, like a lotus flower torn from its root, though the threads will always unite their hearts." Then, in Mandarin she asked me, 'Do you eat apples, Mr Bencoolen?'

'Yes.'

Firmly, without a trace of irony, she said, 'Reflect on this episode of your life by asking: do you cultivate the apple or does the apple cultivate you?'

She leaned in close enough for me to smell the sweat on her brow, feel her breath on my neck, and held the wrapped package to my nose. 'This is the handle of a scythe that must be ever so carefully guarded by people who appreciate its power.'

Up and gone, though she paused at the doorway long enough to leave me with a threat in English: 'You should consider yourself a very lucky man, Mr Bencoolen. You came as close to the apple as you will ever get, and yet you live.'

Then she was gone in a single swirling swish.

Alone, before I blacked out again, my mind flipped through memories of what I'd seen of Chinese religion: the hard clicking of the abacus; the sortilege of thrown bones under the impassive gaze of the flammable blue-faced cipher of the seventh lunar month, the month of burning paper and oranges, the offerings to Hungry Ghosts. And I thought of the indecipherable cat's paw print of the Chinese character, and the delicate hardness of the pearl, and I imagined pearls and apple blossoms woven into the black silk of her hair, and I recalled the words *the bitter apple, and the bite in the apple*, and I knew that I'd been well and truly swindled.

I never did return to Southeast Asia.

William L. Gibson is a writer and educator based in Southeast Asia. His non-fiction book *Art and Money in the Writing of Tobias Smollett* was published in 2007.

In 2009, in collaboration with the record label Sublime Frequencies, he produced a compilation release of original 1960s Chinese-Singapore pop music.

Singapore Black, the first in a trilogy of hard-boiled crime novels set in 1890s Malaya, is published by Monsoon Books.

Author Copyrights

Contribute to Crime Scene Asia

Crime Scene Asia is a print and ebook series with an ongoing call for submissions for crime fiction shorts set in Asia by published and unpublished authors based anywhere in the world. For more information, please visit the the publisher's website at: *www.monsoonbooks.com.sg/submissions*.